RWBY

ROMAN HOLIDAY

RWBY

ROMAN HOLIDAY

E. C. MYERS

Story by KERRY SHAWCROSS and EDDY RIVAS

Based on the series created by MONTY OUM

Scholastic Inc.

ROOSTER TEETH®

All rights reserved. Published by Scholastic Inc., *Publishers since 1920*. SCHOLASTIC and associated logos are trademarks and/or registered trademarks of Scholastic Inc.

The publisher does not have any control over and does not assume any responsibility for author or third-party websites or their content.

This book is a work of fiction. Names, characters, places, and incidents are either the product of the author's imagination or are used fictitiously, and any resemblance to actual persons, living or dead, business establishments, events, or locales is entirely coincidental.

Library of Congress Cataloging-in-Publication Data available

ISBN 978-1-338-76086-6

1 2021

Printed in the U.S.A. 23

First printing 2021 • Book design by Jeff Shake

Cover illustration by Courtney Brenek

CHAPTER ONE

IMAGINARY FRIENDS

Early in the morning on her eighth birthday, Trivia Vanille chased the wild, pink-haired girl through the still, dark rooms of the mansion.

The quiet time belonged to them.

The best friends often played Tiptoe Tag at night after Mama and Papa went to bed. One of them, who was "it," had to catch the other girl, both of them moving as silently as they could. Not making noise wasn't just part of the game, it was essential, because if anyone heard them, they would have to stop playing.

There were other rules, which they made up as they went along. Trivia caught a flash of bright hair heading into the family room. She wasn't allowed to go in there. But those were her parents' rules, and Neopolitan never cared about those. Trivia darted inside with a sense of dread, just as Neo, in a frilly princess dress as pink as her hair, hopped lightly onto the antique coffee table. Neo raised a white-gloved hand to halt Trivia. Then she leaned over and poked her index finger at the floor. As soon as she touched it, she yanked her hand back, shaking it and blowing on her finger dramatically.

Trivia gasped and jumped backward to the doorway. They were adding a new rule to the game. Her eyebrows rose. *The floor is lava?*

Neopolitan nodded and stepped backward onto the cream-colored couch. She bounced up and down on the cushions the way she wasn't supposed to, a taunting smile on her face.

Trivia backed up several feet into the hall so she could get a running start. She took a deep breath before she dashed and sprang from the threshold to the embroidered Mistrali rug. It slipped beneath her on the smooth floor and she almost tumbled into the lake of molten rock, but she caught her balance at the last moment, arms windmilling comically. It was only safe to stand on things that covered the floor without touching it yourself.

The girls moved around the room in an acrobatic dance. They remained the same distance apart, like mirror images of each other. Neopolitan bounced gracefully from sofa to table to piano bench. Trivia followed more slowly, more cautiously. Less steadily.

Neo crouched on the edge of a console table to allow Trivia to catch up. But when Trivia reached from the arm of a wingback chair to tag her, Neo backflipped out of her grasp—so she missed the girl's ankle and slapped something solid instead.

The vase tipped and rolled. Trivia lunged, but her fingers only brushed against the vase as it went over the edge of the table and plummeted into the darkness.

The floor was not lava. It was hard, made from the oldest red-wood trees of Forever Fall forest. The vase shattered. The sound of tiny glass shards scattering around the room reminded her of rain tinkling against the roof.

The silence, too, had been broken.

Neopolitan, balancing with one foot on an end table, covered her mouth with both hands in shock, her mismatched pink and brown eyes wide.

Trivia froze. Maybe her parents hadn't heard that. She hoped that they hadn't. But the footsteps overhead and then on the stairs, the light filling the house, told her it was just a foolish hope.

Neopolitan twirled around and retreated into the shadows, behind a small mountain of wrapped and ribboned boxes of all shapes and sizes: birthday gifts. Trivia scrambled to find a hiding place of her own. She slipped her small body under the sofa just as the lights came on.

Heavy steps. Her father's slippered feet stomped into view.

Papa sighed. "She broke the Akaibara vase."

"Trivia? Trivia, where are you?" Mama called out.

Trivia folded herself smaller under the sofa, eyeing the door. When she pressed a hand against the hardwood floor, she felt a sharp pain. She gasped. A sliver of glass glinted in her palm. How had one of the fragments ended up here, clear on the other side of the room?

"Sweetheart. It's okay. We aren't mad," her mother went on.

"Get out here right now, young lady." Her father's tone of voice hinted at his barely controlled anger. His feet moved out of view.

"Trivia. Please." Mama's voice trembled. "Jimmy, I'll check the other rooms."

It was her mother's concern that convinced Trivia to come out. She stuck a hand from under the sofa, but before she could emerge, firm hands gripped her ankles and yanked her backward. Her hands squeaked along the floor as she tried to hold on. Her palm left a thin streak of blood in the varnish.

Her father dangled her upside down from her ankles. The brown tulle of her dress gathered around her shoulders. She stared up at her father.

He looked calm, wearing the same poker face that served him so well as city manager for the Vale City Council. But there was rage behind his shadowed eyes. She closed her eyes and covered her face with her hands.

"Why aren't you in bed?" He shook her up and down, punctuating each word.

"Jimmy. That's enough," Mama said.

He dumped her onto the sofa she'd just been sheltering beneath and she sat up, smoothing her dress out anxiously.

Mama knelt beside her and put her hand over hers. "What happened?"

Trivia shook her head.

"If you're ever going to speak up for yourself, now is the time," Papa said. "Say something, anything, and we'll forget any of this happened."

Trivia opened her mouth. She wanted to tell him, but the words didn't come. All she could manage was a horrible rasping sound, like she was gasping for breath. Her throat tightened. Her eyes burned with tears. She clamped her mouth shut and shook her head.

He tossed up his hands. "What are we going to do with her?"

Mama stood and retrieved Trivia's communication board from

the coffee table. She handed it to her daughter. "What were you doing down here? How did the vase break?"

Trivia glanced at the empty spot behind the pile of presents. Mama turned to follow her gaze.

"You came to sneak a look at your birthday gifts?" she asked.

Trivia shook her head and slapped the communication board in frustration. With shaking fingers, she moved three letters around on the board. She held it up to show her mother.

"N-E-O," Mama read. "So your 'friend' broke the vase." The weariness in her voice had nothing to do with the late hour.

"Don't encourage her, Carmel," Papa said. "It's all in her head. Something she makes up to avoid responsibility."

"She just has an overactive imagination," Mama said.

"It isn't normal."

"Don't use that word," Mama whispered harshly. "Dr. Mazarin says we have to give her space."

"She has plenty of space. This is what we get for it." He gestured at the broken glass on the floor. "That was an expensive accident."

"It's only money." Her mother's voice had a cutting edge to it.

"And the things I have to do for that money. For my family." He shook his head and looked upward. "Clean this up." His order didn't seem to be directed to anyone in particular. He left the room.

Mama sat next to Trivia on the sofa and put an arm around her. Trivia snuggled in. Her fluttering heartbeat slowed, and she soon started to get sleepy.

"Talk to me," Mama said softly. "Please."

Trivia's eyes snapped open. She stiffened in her mother's embrace.

"You know, Trivia, a friend who does something bad and then leaves you to take the blame isn't a good friend. Is she?" Mama brushed Trivia's hair away from her face. Trivia looked into her mother's big brown eyes and was disappointed when her mother flinched and looked away.

Trivia edged to the side of the couch and crossed her arms. Her mother's expression hardened. She stood abruptly. "Fine. Clean this mess and go to your room. Go to sleep."

Mama walked away. She paused in the doorway and stared at the spot where Neopolitan had been. "Be careful of the sharp pieces. I don't want you to get hurt." She left Trivia in the room. Alone. Again.

Trivia picked at the sliver of glass protruding from her palm. The bright red spots on her finger and thumb blurred from the tears in her eyes. When she had gotten the shard out, she wiped her bloody hand on the cream-colored couch. She picked up the communication board from the floor. The "E" had tumbled off, transforming "Neo" into "No."

Trivia heard glass crunching. Neopolitan was stomping on the remnants of the vase, her hands balled into fists. Trivia waved for her to stop. Neo put her hands on her hips and glared at her.

Trivia knew it was wrong, but she felt angry, too. And that had looked like such fun. She hesitantly stretched out a foot and placed her shoe over a chunk of glass. Neo clapped.

Trivia slowly pressed down. The glass splintered satisfyingly under the heel of her shoe. She kept pushing and turning her heel, grinding the glass into dust. Neo sauntered out of the room, hands clasped behind her back.

Trivia looked down at the mess she'd made, which Papa had told her to clean up. She shrugged and followed Neopolitan again, back to her room. Someone else would pick up the broken pieces later.

CHAPTER TWO

LIE

Roman Torchwick sat on a bench in Sakura Park, huddled behind a crumpled, day-old newspaper. He was pretending to read under the flickering lantern, but he was really keeping an eye on the swanky nightclub across the street—always looking for opportunity.

As with everything in the city of Mistral, the Luck of the Mountains was more than it seemed. You went there for the live music and overpriced, watered-down drinks, you stayed for the illegal gambling in the hidden basement.

Or maybe people just liked the entertainment.

The star attraction of the club, Honey Wine, was to die for—or at least she was capable of leading you to your death. She had a powerful Semblance, one of those special abilities some people had that often seemed like magic. Her sultry voice had an intoxicating effect on others, especially when she sang. It lowered people's inhibitions and made them feel good, even while they were being taken for everything they had. Just the brief snatches of song Roman caught whenever the door opened filled him with longing for something he couldn't put a name to, and conviction that he would find it in the club.

That was why he was hanging out on the other side of the street, so the music didn't lure him inside like the hapless pedestrians who passed by the club—or tried to. As beautiful as Wine and her voice were, Roman planned to keep a safe distance from both of them. Though he was only eighteen years old, he'd already heard enough empty promises in his life.

Ah, another red-faced sucker was stumbling out of the club now. His green overcoat looked expensive and comfortable. Warm. And just about Roman's size.

He wanted that coat. Winter had come to Mistral, and the nights were getting colder. At this rate, he would freeze before he starved to death, but it would be a close race to the end.

More than that, Roman was itching for action. He'd had enough of sitting around waiting for something to happen. He needed to be out there, *making* things happen. He dropped the newspaper to the ground and grabbed his wooden cane as he got up to follow his mark.

The man just missed getting hit by a car as he crossed toward the park side of the street. He was the perfect victim: disoriented and oblivious, wealthy and stupid. Roman altered his course to leave the park and cross paths with the man just as he would pass the exit.

Roman's timing was impeccable. He roughly bumped into the man, using the brief, distracting moment of contact to lift his wallet with him none the wiser.

"Watch it," the man muttered, and stumbled on toward the stairs leading to the upper levels. The city elevator didn't come down this far, to keep more of a buffer between the haves and have nots. It was your business if you wanted to engage in illegal activities in Mistral Below, and people from the base of the mountain had no business topside.

"I sure will," Roman said cheerfully.

This guy was one of those snobs who spent his nights and his money on the lower levels, but had no respect for the people who actually lived there, like Roman. That sort of attitude was one of the things that made the rich so easy to steal from: They held their noses so high, they didn't notice what was right under them.

Pickpocketing was low risk with a high reward, only this time it wasn't Roman's main goal. Aside from identification and credit cards, the wallet only contained a few Lien, as he had anticipated. At Luck of the Mountains, the house always won. The man might have been lulled into buying too many drinks, or he'd had a bad night at the tables. Which was about to get worse.

Roman waited until the man had just turned the corner onto a less busy street and then hurried after him. The man weaved back and forth unsteadily on the road. When he reached the entrance to one of the many blind alleys Mistral was famous for, Roman called after him. "Excuse me! You dropped this!"

The man whirled around, alarmed. The sight of Roman waving his wallet, a friendly and urgent look on his face, put him more at ease. The man patted his pockets. Surprise turned to dismay.

"Where did you get that?" he asked.

"I found it back by the club." Roman held the wallet out. The man grabbed for it, but Roman yanked it back out of reach just before he could take it.

"Hey, it's getting kind of cold. Think you could help a fella out?" Roman asked.

The man scowled. "I bet you stole that from me in the first place."

Roman sighed. "Instead of being rewarded for a good deed, I get accused of committing a crime. What is this world coming to?"

"I've dealt with people like you before. I'm not falling for your con. Return my property or I'll summon the authorities."

"Fine. Here you go." Roman extended his hand with the wallet, and then casually tossed it into the dark alley. "Oops," he said.

The man glanced from Roman to the alley. He sized Roman up: a tall, scrawny teenager with his dirty orange hair tied back in a ragged ponytail. Roman knew he probably didn't seem like much of a threat. But that had worked in his favor plenty of times.

The man turned away from him and went for the bait.

Roman looked around to make sure there was no one else nearby and then followed him into the alley. The man stooped to pick up his wallet. When he stood up, Roman walloped him in the back with his cane.

The man went down and face-planted on the grungy cobble-stones. Another thing that made the rich such good targets: They didn't know how to fight.

The man moaned and rolled over, blinking and confused.

"That's a lovely coat." Roman twirled his cane casually but menacingly. He had practiced the move for hours in front of a cracked mirror he had dragged to his shelter under the Switchback Ridge suspension bridge.

The man started scrambling backward away from Roman, deeper into the dark alley. The only light was from the windows of the buildings on either side. A shadow passed in front of one of them, and then the light went out. The occupants were clearly used to the kinds of things that happened in this alley and were smart enough to want no part of it.

"Don't crawl around like that. You're getting my coat dirty," Roman said.

The man pulled the coat tighter around him. His eyes darted back and forth, looking for help or a way out. "You can't have my coat."

"Don't be a fool. You probably have a closet full of coats at home. You can buy a new one tomorrow." Roman snapped his fingers. "Like that."

The man's expression shifted, showing Roman's words had hit home. The man was weighing the cost of protecting something he wouldn't even miss.

The man jumped up and pushed past Roman with surprising speed and force, screaming "Help! Help!"

Roman sighed. Why did they always run? Why did they expect someone to come to their rescue?

In Mistral, everyone minded their own business—unless knowing other people's business *was* their business. It was the only way to survive. If someone did hear the man's cries, they would be sure to head in the opposite direction, grateful that whatever was going on wasn't happening to them.

Roman had learned that lesson early on, a year ago when he had first come to the city. He had helped a woman he'd thought was being mugged, taking a beating from her attacker before driving him off. Then *Roman* had been arrested, and the ungrateful "victim" fingered him for the crime. It turned out she was a criminal, too. Roman had interrupted a shady deal that went wrong. But she took advantage of the chance to shift attention away from herself by accusing Roman of a crime he didn't commit.

He wouldn't make that mistake again. On the streets, on your own. You only watched out for yourself. Anything else was a weakness. Anyone else was a liability.

Roman drew his cane back and hurled it after the man like a javelin. It traveled true, tripping him and sending him sprawling just short of the alley's entrance. Roman walked over and picked up his cane. He loomed over the man. The man stared up at him with frightened eyes.

"Please. Don't," the man said.

"What exactly do you think I'm going to do?" Roman raised his cane, gripping the shaft like a club. He advanced slowly. The man's eyes focused on the blunt instrument.

It would be a shame to get blood on such a pretty coat. But as long as none of it was his, Roman would call it a win.

"Have you ever wondered what it feels like to be a punching bag?" Roman asked.

The man unbuttoned the coat with fumbling fingers. "Here! It's yours!" He shrugged it off and threw it at Roman.

Roman caught it with the hook of his cane and swirled it around before taking it. He put it on over his threadbare black shirt. The coat was a little roomy, but it made him feel like a million bucks.

"I'll have the gloves, too," Roman said. "If you please."

"You're kidding."

Roman tapped his cane against the ground sharply. "Am I laughing?"

The man peeled his black gloves off.

"Don't throw them. Hand them to me," Roman said.

The man raised a shaking hand. Roman took the gloves. He slipped them on. Leather. Still warm.

"Can I go?" The man shivered.

"Just one last thing." Roman brought his cane back and whipped it down into the man's knee. *Crack!*

The man screamed and writhed on the ground, clutching his leg.

"Tough break." Roman sneered. He watched the man crawl away slowly, whimpering.

"Well, well, well. What do we have here, Mortar?" A deep voice came from outside the alley.

"Looks like another young punk stealing from innocent citizens, Brick." A higher-pitched voice.

Here we go, Roman thought. He sauntered out onto the road, figuring he'd had the bad fortune to attract the attention of a couple of goody-goody Huntsmen. He nearly laughed when he saw the two men, one tall and broad shouldered, the other short and boxy. They wore purple outfits and sported spider-and-cobweb tattoos identifying them as members of Lil' Miss Malachite's organization.

That's the kind of place Mistral was, where the *gangsters* wore uniforms and enforced their own rule of law.

He recognized these goons. Once a week, they came around Peddlers Row to collect a tribute from the shops there. They always ended their night at Luck of the Mountains. And since they stayed for a few hours, Roman figured not all of the kickbacks they collected were making it back to Lil' Miss.

"What's so funny?" Brick asked. His cheeks and forehead flushed with angry splotches of red.

"For a second, I was worried you boys were Huntsmen." Roman chuckled. Mortar laughed along with him until Brick smacked him on the back of the head.

"You're that thief we've been looking for," Brick said.

"I'm flattered. It's nice to feel wanted," Roman said. "Not by the police, of course." He eyed the two gangsters. He might be in trouble here. But if he could beat them, the protection money they were carrying would get him a nicer place to stay. He could buy warmer clothes. Stop eating cheap street noodles for every meal. Take a shower. Maybe even move into a place with a roof and four walls.

"If you steal from patrons, you're stealing from the club. If you're stealing from the club, you're stealing from Lil' Miss Malachite."

"You have a unique grasp of socioeconomics," Roman said. He tightened his grip on his cane's handle. Brick and Mortar had only guns and muscles, but they might have other tricks up their sleeves. Roman gave himself a 70 percent chance of winning a fight against them.

He would never place a bet at Luck of the Mountains, but he wasn't afraid to gamble when the odds were in his favor.

"No one operates around here without Lil' Miss's blessing. And you owe her back pay for everything you've taken so far," Mortar said.

"I don't need Malachite's 'protection,'" Roman said.

"We'll see about that." The taller one, Brick, rushed forward. Roman sidestepped him easily, whacking him in the butt with his cane and sending him head over heels. Roman whirled around and swung his cane, knocking the gun out of Mortar's hand as he fired. The bullet missed Roman by a hair.

Roman spun his cane around in one hand to hook the handle around Mortar's wrist. He pulled and stepped back, steering him into Brick, who was just standing up again. They both went down in a tangle of limbs and curses.

"We've got a funny guy here," Brick said.

"You two are the jokes," Roman said. "I'm just the punch line." Gripping each end of his cane, he bashed Brick in the face with its shaft.

Brick shook it off quickly and pulled his gun. Roman jabbed at his chest with the tip of his cane, pushing him backward. But then Mortar tackled Roman's legs and he fell on his back, trying to kick the little guy off. Brick grabbed for his cane, but Roman held on to it. His opponent changed his tactic, pushing the weapon against Roman's neck. Choking him.

With a bellow, Roman pushed hard and then pulled, unbalancing the ungentle giant. Roman knocked his forehead into Brick's and the man collapsed on him, unconscious. Roman nearly blacked out himself, but he held it together and blinked away the dots flashing in his vision.

Roman rolled Brick off him and looked around. Mortar was gone.

Just as he'd always figured, Lil' Miss's men were just your run-of-the-mill thugs. Bullies who didn't amount to much when they were challenged.

Roman checked Brick's pockets and came up with a thick

envelope stuffed with Lien. He would not be eating noodles tonight.

It took the Spider gang two days to find him. He heard them outside his room at the Happenstance Hotel a moment before they opened the door—with a key. He steeled himself for a fight until he saw that Brick and Mortar had brought ten of their strongest friends, all in the same purple garb.

Lil' Miss Malachite had sent a small army after him.

"What took you gents so long?" Roman asked. With Malachite's connections—to everyone, it seemed—they should have found him much sooner. It might be over, but he'd enjoyed two days of the good life, with a full stomach and luxurious baths and sleeping in a real bed again. Worth it.

"Lil' Miss wants a word with you," Brick growled.

"What if I don't want a word with her?" Roman asked.

"What you want doesn't matter. Your life belongs to her."

Lil' Miss Malachite wasn't what he'd expected. When the Spiders dragged Roman into her tavern, she was seated in the back, neat stacks of Lien on the table before her. She was in her thirties with short blond hair and a beauty mark on one rosy cheek. Lil' Miss was renowned for having a strategic mind, which applied to her fashion choices as well. Her white-and-purple dress showed off bare shoulders, drawing the eye to a tattoo of a spider in a web on the left shoulder; a plunging neckline and purple corset distracted Roman even more. She puffed on a cigarette in a holder while she studied Roman with piercing blue eyes.

"You've been busy, boy," she said.

"I'm not a boy," he said.

"You ain't a man, neither, not by a far sight." She knocked some ash from her cigarette into a purple ashtray at her elbow. "You know what that makes you?"

"What?"

"You're just *potential*. You're caught between what you were and what you could be. This is that crucial time where you can decide who you want to be."

Roman raised his eyebrows. She really wasn't anything like he'd imagined. He couldn't fathom how she'd overthrown the old boss of the Spider organization and taken over, or how she was able to operate so successfully under the watchful eye of the Mistral City Council. But here she was: arguably the most powerful person in the city, outside of Leonardo Lionheart, headmaster of the Huntsmen Academy, Haven.

"This is the guy who's been stealing from us, ma'am," Mortar said.

Lil' Miss waved her hand. "What do you have to say about that, Mr. . . .?"

"Torchwick. Roman Torchwick. And ma'am, I think that says more about your Spiders than it does about me. I've just been doing what we all do—try to survive."

"All you want is to *survive*? I'm disappointed. You seem like one of those ambitious types who always want more than they've got." She smiled. "I'm like that, too."

"Ma'am, when you don't have anything, surviving *is* more. You've gotta start somewhere. If I were you, I'd be more disappointed in Brick and Mortar here."

"Shut your mouth!" Brick said.

"Do *not* shut that pretty little mouth of yours," Lil' Miss said. "I sure do want to hear this." She glared at Brick, and Roman didn't want her to ever look at him like that.

Roman gave her a lopsided grin. "Here I am, a *boy*, and I just about bested two of your Spiders. And everyone knows it. It took a dozen of them to bring me in—and I only cooperated because I wanted to meet you.

"With all due respect, your crew is a disgrace. If they can lose to me when it's two against one, how can they intimidate anyone? How can you trust them to get the job done?"

"You think you could do better?" Brick growled.

"With my eyes closed," Roman said.

"Let's test that right now." Brick rolled up his sleeves.

Lil' Miss held up a hand. "*Could* you do better, Mr. Torchwick? Truly?"

Roman paused. "I couldn't do any worse."

"You really must set your sights a bit higher. Show more *fire*, if you want to live up to your name." The tip of her cigarette glowed bright orange as she took a drag of it. "All right. You work for me now."

"Ma'am?" Roman, Brick, and Mortar spoke at the same time.

"I like your confidence, but they're just empty words if you can't back them up with action. Like I said, I see a lot of potential in you, Torchwick."

"You should have seen him!" Mortar spoke up. "He's vicious. He brutally beat a man just for his coat. He was having *fun*."

"That so? Well, I've always felt it was important for one to love their work if you want them to be good at it," Lil' Miss said. "And if it's that coat he's wearing, he also has good taste."

"Do I have a choice?" Roman asked. "I tend to work better alone." He couldn't believe his luck being invited into the biggest crime organization this side of Lake Matsu, but he wanted to play it cool. Although it was probably pointless to try to bluff someone who could see through him so clearly.

"We always have a choice, but I can't let you walk after stealing from me."

"So I join you or . . ."

She nodded. "Or." She tapped her cigarette into the ashtray. She used the cigarette as a prop, to punctuate her words and redirect attention. He appreciated her dangerous, dramatic flair.

Roman swallowed. "Then I'm honored to accept."

"Yes, you are. And now we'll find out after all what you can do with your eyes closed."

Roman frowned. "How's that?"

"They'll probably be swollen shut for a couple days, once Brick is through with you. Call it a punishment; call it an initiation. Either way, you've got it coming and you are going to take your licks."

Lil' Miss nodded to Brick.

This was all a mistake, Roman thought as he watched Brick advance toward him, cracking his knuckles.

But Roman was good at learning from his mistakes, no matter how painful they were. As long as he survived to make another one later.

CHAPTER THREE

PAINTING THE TOWN PINK

Despite living in Vale her whole life, all twelve years of it, Trivia had never seen the commercial district at night before. She had only been there shopping for clothes, books, and toys with her mother, whenever Papa sent them out so he could "take care of business in peace" at home. Whatever that meant. And she was never, ever allowed out alone. "For your own safety," they said.

The city in the evening was like a different world, as magical as one of her favorite fairy tales. She'd had no idea so many businesses were open this late; all their lights almost made it as bright as day. She only caught glimpses of the broken full moon between the towering buildings. And there were *so many people*—strolling and shopping; couples holding hands while walking; groups of kids just hanging out, taking pictures of each other with their Scrolls and uploading them and not doing anything in particular.

It was so beautiful; it almost hurt.

I love this, she thought.

Neopolitan nudged her with an elbow and raised her eyebrows, a combination of *I told you so* and *You haven't seen anything yet*.

Trivia had been worried about sneaking out during her parents' big party. Papa was celebrating a major new business contract he had closed, and Trivia wasn't invited. They had ordered her to stay in her room, where she found a box of new video games to distract her. They insisted she would be dreadfully bored being around all those stuffy adults, but she knew the truth.

They were ashamed of her. Because she couldn't speak. Because of her mismatched eyes. On the rare occasions that she did go out with them, they made her wear a brown contact lens over her pink eye.

Trivia was good at staying low and staying quiet—ha ha. And she had planned on doing as she was told, hiding in her room, out of sight. Out of mind. But the music and the laughter and the aroma of delicious food had gotten to her. Then Neo had a brilliant, terrible idea: They wanted Trivia to stay out of the way, so why not leave the house?

Even her bedroom had grown too confining and she couldn't run around the house playing with Neo, but there was a whole wide city out there to explore. She would be back before the party was over, Neo assured her, and her parents would never even miss her.

So she put on her "adventuring outfit," a white tank top, a brown blazer and pants, and her favorite white sneakers with the pink hearts. Simply leaving her room felt like a transgression and she almost stopped there, but Neo shoved her into the hall. The loud conversation of the party guests nearly drowned out the expensive live band. Such a waste.

Each step through the house toward the back door emboldened her, Neo pushing her on and on and on until she was outside. She was frightened but exhilarated, like she was coming alive for the first time.

Everything was a new, exciting, scary experience: riding the bus across town, sitting on a fountain in the square and watching people go by. Trivia had no particular destination and no goal other than to see as much as she could before she had to go back to her normal, sheltered life. To live as much as she could, making up for lost time and because she didn't know when she would get another chance at freedom.

Of all the wondrous things in Vale, including the arcades, bookshops, and movie theaters, Trivia's absolute favorite thing was the food carts. They sold food right there on the street, as if every day was the Vytal Festival. And you could get anything you wanted: popcorn, cakes, burgers, milkshakes. Fresh-baked cookies the size of a plate, sugar-spun candy, ice-cream sundaes bigger than her head, steaming baskets of fries with a dozen different dipping sauces. Trivia wanted it all, but she settled on a chocolate-and-vanilla shake to start.

Neo looked on jealously while Trivia took her first sip. Heavenly. The perfect balance of flavor and just the right consistency.

"What's wrong with your eye?" a voice said.

Trivia frowned and looked at a girl with green streaks in her short, spiky hair. She was flanked by two other girls, who had similar hair and identical outfits: short-sleeved black jackets, pale blue tops, tight miniskirts with silver chain belts, chunky boots. Was this a gang?

The girls were only a few years older than Trivia, maybe fifteen or sixteen, and she envied them for being out on their own and for dressing and styling their hair however they wanted.

"And *what* is she wearing?" another girl said in a singsong voice. "Look at those shoes!"

Trivia's face grew warm.

"She's just a little kid," the third girl said softly.

"Nobody asked you, *Heather*." The girl rolled her eyes.

Trivia lowered her head and turned to go, but the first girl stepped in her way. "Hey, where you going? We just want to talk."

Trivia touched her throat and shook her head.

"You don't want to talk to us?" The other girls giggled. She held up a hand and they stopped. "I get it. You aren't supposed to talk to strangers. Well, I'm Cookie. This is Mags and—" She sighed. "Heather. You can hang out with us, if you buy us shakes, too."

"I'll take butterscotch," Mags said.

"Mint chip for me," Cookie said.

"I'm good," Heather said.

Neo stalked around them, hands behind her back, a scowl on her face. Trivia followed her with her eyes.

"Come on, what's your name?" Cookie said. "Don't you want to be friends? Friends don't let friends go out dressed like that. Hey, how about after the shakes, we can go clothes shopping."

Trivia shook her head again and tried to shove past Cookie, but the girl pushed her back. "I didn't say you could go."

Trivia narrowed her eyes. Neo made fists and jabbed with her left, then her right, in the girl's direction.

"Just leave her alone," Heather said. "Let's go see a movie."

"Sure, whatever." Cookie stepped aside and swept out an arm to let Trivia leave.

Trivia hurried away, but as she passed Cookie, the girl tripped her. She landed on her hands and knees. Her shake spattered everywhere, all over her clothes.

Trivia stood up. Cookie and Mags were laughing and pointing at her. She blinked back tears. Her throat got tight.

A crack appeared in the ground between her and the girls. They screamed and stumbled backward as the fissure grew wider.

"Watch out!" Cookie shouted.

"What's happening?" Mags said.

Heather studied Trivia from the other side of the gap. "Did you do that?"

Trivia glanced behind the trio. They turned and saw Neopolitan there, her pink hair now in the same style as the clique and in matching pink-and-white clothes.

"What do *you* want?" Cookie asked. "Don't tell me you're friends with her."

They could see Neo?

Her parents had been catching glimpses of Neopolitan lately when Trivia was upset, which was more and more often these days, but she couldn't make her as solid as the smaller, inanimate illusions she pranked them with around the house. Creating another person was much more difficult than a vase of dried-up roses, a broken step, or a bloodstain on the sofa. So her friend only lived in her head—until now. It seemed that everyone could see her. Of course seeing was one thing, but touching—

Neopolitan smiled and punched Cookie in the face. Neo's hand shattered like glass, the impact rippling through her arm and breaking apart the rest of her body until the shards faded, along with the illusory crack in the ground.

But it wasn't all an illusion. Cookie's hand was over her nose, blood gushing from between the fingers.

Trivia was almost as shocked as the girls were. She hadn't created anything with her Semblance as big as that crack before—or two separate illusions at the same time.

"Whoa," Heather said.

"Freak!" Mags shrieked.

Cookie moaned and blubbered. The front of her pretty blue shirt was ruined, splattered with blood.

Trivia suddenly noticed the small crowd gathered around them. Some people were holding up their Scrolls taking pictures. She backed up slowly, people parting to make way for her.

A siren blared and red and blue lights flashed. A black-and-white police car rolled up to the curb. A cop stepped out. "What's going on here?"

Trivia spun on her heels and ran.

"Hey," the cop said. "Hey! Stop!"

Oh no oh no oh no. I'm in big trouble. Trivia ran as fast as she could, the police siren blaring behind her. The flashing lights following her, casting her long shadow ahead of her.

"Stop!" a voice blared on the car's speaker.

Trivia abruptly changed direction and darted down another street, only to find the end of it blocked by a chain-link fence and construction signs. She heard a sharp whistle and looked up. Neopolitan was balancing on top of the fence, back in her own pink-and-white adventure outfit. She gestured for Trivia to jump up.

Easy for you to say, Trivia thought. *I'll have to do this the hard way.*

She started climbing, but it wasn't as easy as it looked on TV. She had almost reached the top when she felt a hand close around her ankle.

"That's enough. Come down here, kid."

Trivia held on tight, the metal wire biting into her fingers. She looked over her shoulder and pulled on her leg, trying to shake his hand free.

"Think about it, where are you going to go?" The cop pointed at the big hole in the ground on the other side of the fence with bare girders rising from it high above the ground. "Please don't make me follow you. I'm afraid of heights."

Trivia sighed. She let go. The cop caught her and lowered her gently to her feet.

"Now what's going on?" the cop asked her. "Why'd you run?"

Trivia pulled out her Scroll to type out a response, but he grabbed it from her. "Hey. Answer me."

She opened her mouth, but all that came out was a sob. She swiped at her eyes, embarrassed that she was crying. She was so tired. She sat down, right there in the dirt.

The cop crouched. "It's all right. It's going to be all right. What's your name?"

Trivia pointed at the Scroll, then opened her mouth and pointed at her open mouth.

"You want to make a call?" he asked.

"She can't talk." His partner, a woman with graying hair and kind eyes, took the Scroll and returned it to Trivia.

Trivia smiled gratefully. She typed furiously and then showed them the screen.

I didn't do anything. Not my fault.

"Those girls have gotten in trouble before, so I believe it. That's why we were parked nearby. But you were involved in some kind of disturbance," the male cop said. His badge read "Arad."

"But it kind of seems like *you* were the victim here?" The woman's badge identified her as Officer Cloud. "Let's just get you home. What's your name?"

Trivia typed. **Trivia Vanille.**

"Vanille? As in Jimmy Vanille? I didn't even know he had a daughter," Cloud said.

Trivia shrugged and spread her hands. *Here I am.*

"Hey, maybe there'll be a reward for bringing her home," Arad said.

His partner bopped him on the head. "Dum-dum."

Trivia sat in the back of the patrol car, head down, unable to look out at the city as they drove her home.

"Still no answer." Cloud put down her Scroll.

"Maybe they're out looking for her," Arad said.

Trivia rolled her eyes. Then she noticed Cloud watching her in the rearview mirror. Trivia closed her eyes and folded her arms.

The party was still in full swing when the car pulled up the driveway to her house. All the windows except Trivia's were lit, and lively music filled the air.

Arad whistled. "No wonder they didn't answer."

"That's still no excuse," Cloud said sullenly. "I'd like to say a few things to Trivia's parents."

So would I, Trivia thought.

The circular driveway was jam-packed with partygoers' cars, so Arad double-parked.

"Who's gonna give us a ticket?" he joked.

They escorted Trivia up the pathway to the large double doors of the front entrance. She dragged her feet more as they got closer.

"Anything you want to tell me before we ring that doorbell?" Cloud asked Trivia softly. When she saw Trivia's exasperated look, she apologized. "Just nod or shake your head. Are they treating you okay?"

Trivia hesitated for just a split second, but she nodded.

"Have they ever hit you?"

Trivia shook her head.

"Do you feel safe here?"

Trivia tipped her head to the side thoughtfully. Before she could respond, the door flew open and Carmel Vanille stepped outside. She pulled the door almost all the way closed behind her. Trivia saw men in tuxedos and women in sparkling evening dresses milling around behind her.

"Can I help you, off—" Mama caught sight of Trivia and her eyes rounded. "Trivia! What have you done?"

"Don't worry, she's all right," Officer Cloud said. "And she isn't in any trouble. We picked her up downtown. She got into a little fight—"

"A *fight?*" Mama shot Trivia a penetrating look. Trivia shrugged.

"You will explain all this later, and hope your father doesn't find out you've been out." Mama glanced behind her, as though afraid he would come to the door and find them standing out here. Or that a guest would notice her speaking to the police.

"So you didn't know your daughter was out?" Cloud asked.

"I had no idea. As you can see, we're rather busy tonight. Trivia was up in her room, or so I thought."

Just like Neo had promised: They hadn't missed her at all. If she hadn't gotten mixed up with those girls and used her Semblance in front of strangers, she could have gotten back home without them being the wiser. The thought was as comforting as it was depressing.

Something bad could have happened to her tonight, and they never would have known that, either. They probably would have blamed her, too, when they found out.

"We'll let you get back to your party, but we may follow up with you later," Arad said.

"Thank you," Mama said. She turned her attention to Trivia. "Get inside. Go around to the servants' entrance and straight up to your room. We'll discuss this before bed. To save us some time at the end of a very long night, write down what you did and just what you were thinking."

Arad and Cloud exchanged a look.

Trivia started to head for the servants' entrance when she caught sight of Neopolitan inside, her pink hair pulled up away from her neck, and wearing a shimmery black-and-white gown and long white gloves. She winked at Trivia and beckoned her inside with a finger.

Trivia glanced up at her mom. She took a breath. And she pushed past her, through the door, into the foyer.

"Trivia! Get back here!" Mama called.

Trivia ignored her and followed Neo as she weaved through the crowd. Her parents didn't want anyone to see Trivia. They didn't pay enough attention to her to know when she was gone. Well, they couldn't miss her now.

Trivia strategically bumped into guests to make them spill their drinks, drop their plates. She flexed her Semblance a tiny bit, creating a mouse that scampered from under a table and up a man's trousers. He yelled and shook his leg frantically while his wife beat at the mouse with her purse.

Earlier, Trivia had been too startled to enjoy the new things she could do with her Semblance. Her parents had always punished her for using the power, warned her to keep it a secret. They'd been holding her back. What else could she do if she continued developing her ability?

As Trivia marched through the middle of the party, she waved her hand and set flies buzzing around the musicians' heads, sending the song they were playing wildly off-tune. A woman found an eyeball floating in her champagne flute and flung it away from her, drenching another guest and breaking the glass.

Trivia stopped for a second in the midst of the chaos she was creating and smiled. Then she saw Papa staring from across the room, jaw set and face purple with rage. Only he wasn't staring at Trivia—his eyes were fixed on Neopolitan. He was furious.

Suddenly afraid, Trivia released her illusions. As Neo faded, she curtsied to Jimmy Vanille. And he turned his anger toward his daughter.

Trivia trembled under his seething gaze. She had felt so strong and carefree a moment ago, but she had forgotten there would be consequences for sneaking out, disobeying her mother, disrupting their party. For showing off her Semblance outside of the family. There would be questions and rumors and Papa would have to pay to make them go away.

Trivia cried for the second time that evening. *What am I doing? What have I done?*

She couldn't just make a mess and fade away like Neo, without taking responsibility. When Neo had punched Cookie, Trivia was the one the cops took away. She was the one the girls blamed.

It wasn't me! It was her. Neo had encouraged Trivia to sneak out and to walk into the party. But Neo was part of her, so did that mean it really was Trivia doing all those awful things?

She shook her head, trying to clear the confusion she felt. Deep down, she didn't regret a moment of what had happened that night and she wanted to do even more—and worse. She was proud of herself.

That had to be Neo's influence again. Trivia had to stay in control. And to start with, she needed to apologize for everything. She would explain it to Papa, make him understand that she hadn't meant any of it and it would never happen again. She took a shaky step toward her father.

He shook his head slowly, his eyes stern. He pressed his lips together and pointed up the stairs.

Trivia turned and fled to her room.

CHAPTER FOUR

STEAL

"Is that another stupid get-rich-quick scheme? Heist Plan Number Seventeen . . ." Brat #1, otherwise known as Melanie Malachite, peered over Roman's shoulder at the notebook he was writing in.

"I'm impressed." Roman snapped his notebook shut.

"Because . . .?"

"I didn't think you knew how to read."

"You're mixing me up with Miltia again," she said in a bored voice. She always sounded bored, but this time she had a reason to be after spending more than a week in lockdown.

"Hey. I can read, I just choose not to." Her twin sister, Brat #2, a.k.a. Miltiades, went back to watching a Faunus soap opera.

He was glad for the reminder of which was which, because it really was hard to tell them apart, especially when they wore the same outfit: purple halter tops, black cut-off shorts, and mid-calf boots.

They say that the reward for doing a good job is it becomes your job permanently. Four years after he had joined the Spiders, Roman was now Lil' Miss Malachite's right-hand man, only partially because he was one of the few gang members to survive in one piece. So he was the only one she trusted to protect her daughters during one of the worst wars among the crime organizations that Mistral had ever seen.

Roman's reward for being the best was holing up in a safe house with two snotty, apathetic, spoiled teenage girls. He should be out there tracking down members of rival organizations, but instead he was forced to be a glorified babysitter.

"I assume plans one through sixteen failed." Melanie sat down across from him at the table. It had finally happened: She was willing to talk to him because she had nothing better to do.

"They haven't failed." Roman flipped through the pages of his notebook. "I'm still . . . planning them."

"So. They haven't failed *yet*," Melanie said.

"You are your mother's daughter," Roman replied. He didn't know who their father was, but he envied him for being smart enough to get as far away from this wacky family as he could.

Then again, he was probably dead. So he was only slightly worse off than Roman.

"What's a 'heist,' anyway?" Miltia asked.

Melanie glanced up to the ceiling in exasperation. "It's a big robbery. Like, a bank or a train."

Roman turned to the page where he had sketched out Heist Plan Number Nine. "The Mistral Trading Company uses the old Zephyr Line to transport Lien from their banks around the Kingdom to Fort Charon." He turned the page. "I have a plan to break into that, too."

"So why haven't you done it yet?" Melanie asked.

"A plan needs people, and as amazing as I am, there's but one of me," Roman said.

"Lil' Miss has plenty of people working for her!" Miltia said. He had never heard the girls call their mother anything but Lil' Miss.

Roman closed his book and tucked it into his coat. "I wouldn't trust any of those goons to pull off one of these jobs."

"You're one of those goons," Melanie said.

"I know why you don't like working with a partner, Roman," Miltia said.

"Oh yeah? Enlighten me," he said.

"You don't like sharing. You want all the profit for yourself."

Roman sniffed. "Sharing profit means sharing the risk. Working with a partner doubles the chance of failure, for half the incentive."

"You just need the right partner," Melanie and Miltia said. As creepy as it was when they finished each other's sentences, it was more disturbing when they said the same thing at the same time.

"Maybe. I just don't believe anyone is going to watch out for me as much as I will," he said. "I'd appreciate it if you didn't tell anyone about my plans. Until they're ready," he said.

He didn't know why he'd told them all that. It was dangerous, underestimating the brats. They might only be thirteen, but they were still Malachites, and Malachites knew how to turn information—even the most innocuous—to their advantage.

Melanie smiled. "Don't worry. Lil' Miss wouldn't be interested in any of your heists, anyway."

Roman narrowed his eyes. "Why not?"

"Stealing money? That's what a goon does. If you want to be a *boss*, you need to think bigger. Where does the money come from?"

"The *bank*." Roman rolled his eyes.

"The banks move the money. But what *makes* the money? What does every Kingdom need?"

"Even I know that one," Miltia said. "Dust."

Dust. Maybe the rugrats had a point. Dust powered everything, everywhere, from planes to trains to automobiles. The Cross Continental Transmit System, the central communication network for all of Remnant, relied on the power it generated, and so did the Scrolls that used the CCT. Even weapons used Dust as fuel, its different forms—fire, ice, electricity, gravity, and many variations and combinations thereof—having different destructive effects.

And if you had a Semblance . . . many people used Dust to enhance their special abilities in some interesting and devastating ways.

The biggest name in Dust was the Atlas-based Schnee Dust Company, but they did business in all four Kingdoms, from mining and storage to commercial distribution and point-of-sales, with many other companies vying for the still extremely lucrative scraps. If Roman could get a piece of that action—

Something yanked Roman's hair and his head was pulled backward by his ponytail.

"Ow! Don't do that, kid," he said.

"Can I braid this?" Miltia asked. "Please?"

"No!"

Miltia grabbed his hat.

"Hey! Do not. Touch. The hat." Roman spun around and grabbed to get it back. Miltia tossed it past him like a disc to Melanie.

"Girls. That is not a toy. Give it back to me, or—"

"Or what? You'll ground us? We've already been stuck in here with you for a *week*. Ugh!" Melanie tossed the hat back to Miltia, just out of his reach.

"Yeah. What are you gonna do? Tell Lil' Miss?" Miltia said.

Roman sighed. On the bright side, the girls clearly needed to burn off a lot of energy, and playing with his hat was literally keeping them out of his hair.

"Right. Fine. What do I care?" He tossed up his hands.

At least they weren't messing with his new cane anymore. Now that Roman had money and resources, he had replaced his old wooden cane with a metal one that not only was strong enough to deflect the sharpest blades and hold up under tremendous force, but also was deadly on both ends. It was equipped with a grappling hook in the handle and a concealed flare gun in the tip that fired—what else—fire Dust. Since causing pain and destruction were music to his ears, he had named it Melodic Cudgel. The only thing he had forgotten to include in the weapon of his dreams was a safety lock, which he realized when Melanie had almost blown off her sister's head the other day.

He wasn't entirely sure that had been an accident.

He needed to get a big score and strike out on his own, preferably before the twins grew up. The brats were a handful now, but they'd be really dangerous when they were older. He hoped they'd get the all clear so they could go home before they injured or killed him, or each other; of course if anything happened to one of them on his watch, it would still be curtains for him.

Roman's Scroll buzzed. It was Chameleon, another associate

of the Spider organization. She wasn't the brightest crayon in the box, but she was the most colorful, on account that her Semblance allowed her to change the color of her skin. This ability could be useful for spy work, but sometimes it worked against Chameleon—and whoever was partnered with her.

You had to trust the people you worked with, and the people who worked for you. So Lil' Miss had set up a buddy system for new recruits, pairing them with members of the organization she already knew were loyal. But not necessarily competent. Word was that getting matched with Chameleon was more a hazing than training. Roman found out why when Lil' Miss ordered the two of them to follow a councilman in the hopes of finding dirt they could use for blackmail or sensitive information to sell.

They had tailed the guy to a meeting with Jack Plum, one of Lil' Miss's rivals who tried to have a finger in every pie in Mistral. The plan was for Roman to cause a distraction outside so Chameleon could use her camouflaging ability to sneak into the room and record their conversation. It turned out she wasn't so good under pressure. When she got nervous, her skin shifted colors uncontrollably, which naturally drew the attention of Plum's guards.

By the time Roman made it to Chameleon, the left side of her face was badly cut up—Plum was notoriously vicious and cruel when he got cornered. Roman barely got the two of them out alive, then he lied to Lil' Miss about another gang breaking up the meeting—more to save his own standing than Chameleon's neck. Though she had certainly suffered enough already at Plum's blades, and would always carry the scars to prove it.

Chameleon read more into Roman's covering for her than she should have. She considered him a friend, and plainly wanted more than that. For his part, Roman considered Chameleon a liability. Semblances were overrated, and one that you couldn't control was worse than none at all. Still, she could be useful on occasion and fun to be around on other occasions, so he continued to string her along. He answered the video call.

"Hey, Cammie, what's up?" He reconsidered. "You're a sight for sore eyes."

Her skin turned bright red. "He's back, Roman," Cammie whispered.

"Who's back? You'll have to be more specific." A lot of gang members were on the lam when tensions ran hot, hiding out like Roman was.

No, *he* wasn't hiding. The girls were laying low and he was protecting them.

"The bird has landed." Cammie's skin transitioned to green.

"Did we agree to use a passcode or something? I must have missed that memo." Roman rubbed his eyes. On the far end of the room, the twins were pretending to be texting on their Scrolls, but they were obviously listening in on his conversation. Maybe speaking in code wasn't such a bad idea.

"I'm talking the big bird in the mouse house." The way the unscarred side of her mouth turned up, he knew she was having him on.

Roman gritted his teeth. "Even I'm not bored enough for your riddles." Then he realized what she was saying. "Oh. Right. Good work. Where is he?"

She turned the same shade of purple as the Spider gang colors. "He's come home to roost."

"I hate you," Roman said.

She blew him a kiss. "In an hour I'm going to tell the big boss what I just told you, but I thought you'd appreciate the heads-up. Looking forward to seeing you again when all this mess clears up."

Roman tried to tip his hat to her, then remembered he wasn't wearing it. "Take care, Cammie."

Roman looked at the time on his Scroll. He had only two hours. Would the girls be okay on their own for a little while? No, Lil' Miss would murder him when she heard about it. Everything would get back to their mother and his boss, sooner rather than later. And if she didn't like how things turned out, he'd be done for.

So if he was going to act on this, he had to involve the twins, and make sure nothing happened to them, *and* his plan had to succeed.

That was a powerful argument to do nothing. But living in a three-room safe house with the twin terrors was making him edgy, too, and he'd do almost anything to go outside.

He pulled out his notebook. "You girls want to hear about Heist Plan Number Eighteen?" He turned to a fresh page and drew. A moment later he held up the book to show it to them.

Melanie peered closer at the two girls he had sketched in a corner of the page. "Are those supposed to be us?"

"They are indeed. We have a once-in-a-lifetime chance to pull off a major job. A legendary job. But I'm going to need help. *Your* help."

"Us?" Miltia asked. "But we're just kids."

Melanie jabbed an elbow into her sister's ribs.

Roman smiled. "That's why it has to be you."

Melanie handed Roman his hat. "We're in."

"You don't want to hear the plan first?"

"I just want to do *something*!"

He put his hat back on. Now he could think better. He gestured for the girls to gather around him while he put his thoughts to paper.

Roman and Melanie waited outside the Parrot & Mouse. They didn't need to knock, and they didn't wait long.

Roman saw the blinds at the front windows twitch and knew they were being watched. The door opened, and Badger, the Parrot gang's bouncer, stepped out. He had his signature pool cue balanced carelessly on his shoulder.

"Well, well, well. Hiya, Torchwick. This your new girlfriend?"

"Ew," Melanie said. "As if."

"You know who it is," Torchwick said.

"Where's the other one? Don't twins usually come in twos?"

"And your pals say you aren't that smart," Torchwick said.

"What?" Badger advanced threateningly, bringing his pool cue around and slapping it in one hand.

"The other brat is close, but safe. She's my insurance," Roman said.

"What are you worried about?"

"That you'll kill me and take both of them hostage."

"How about I kill both of you?"

"Your boss would dislike that almost as much as my boss would. Surely you know that. And if you don't, your backup in there does. You said it yourself: the Malachite girls come as a package deal, and Paul Parrot isn't one to settle for less than a complete set."

Badger flexed the pool cue and glared at Torchwick. But he stepped aside and swung his cue toward the door, gesturing for them to enter.

"I smell a rat," Badger growled. "If you try to pull anything—"

"Keep it down. Your boss isn't a big fan of rodents, if I recall."

"He's got it under control." Badger laughed.

Melanie stomped on the thug's foot as she passed. He bellowed and lunged for her. Roman blocked him with his cane. "She's just a kid, big man."

Melanie stomped on Torchwick's foot next. He clenched his jaw and forced a pained smile. "Girls will be girls. She and her sister will be your problem soon."

Roman had never been inside the Parrot & Mouse before, as it was the headquarters of a rival criminal organization. But he had paid a premium for photos of the tavern and a detailed sketch of the floor plans, so he knew what to expect. Except for the basement. Everyone knew that with the exception of Paul Parrot, anyone who went down there never came back up. Which is why Roman was here. He wanted to see what was in the basement, and Melanie was his ticket.

A few Parrot gang members in green-and-gold suits watched as Badger led Roman and Melanie toward a stairwell leading up. He casually glanced over the room and made note of a door that hadn't been marked on his maps. That had to lead *downstairs*.

The room over the tavern held a big dining table, and behind it sat the crime lord Paul Parrot. The man had deep tan skin, likely because he spent most of his time running small operations on the coastal towns to the north. His greasy black hair was slicked back and he had bushy eyebrows and a hawklike nose. He wore a deep green tuxedo jacket with a yellow bow tie and matching waistcoat, embroidered with an iridescent feather pattern.

Without acknowledging their presence, he picked up a piece of dry toast from his plate and scraped butter and jam across it. Contemplating the toast in his hand, he spoke.

"Roman Torchwick. I should kill you right now. You have been such a pain in my ass. And yet—" He took a bite and chewed thoughtfully. "You've come here with a peace offering."

Roman stepped forward. Badger moved to stop him, but Parrot waved him off. He gestured for Roman to approach.

"You may not believe me, but I'm a big fan of yours," Roman said.

"A big fan of mine? You're right: I don't believe you." Parrot took another bite. Roman hated the crunching sound as he chewed, which was likely why he was doing it. "You work for Lil' Miss Malachite." Crumbs sprayed from his mouth, hitting Roman in the chest. Roman brushed them off.

"I want to work for you." Roman gestured to Melanie. "As you can see, I'm tendering my resignation."

"You want to work for me. So that's what this is. You think you can buy your way into my gang?"

"The ransom you'll get for her and her sister will be more than enough, and you can demand a truce with Lil' Miss. You might even be able to take over her organization. Aren't you tired of this war?"

"It hasn't been good for business, though it has its moments. It reminds me of the old days. When I was a kid, the gangs could get away with anything. Now, we have to be sneakier about it and pay the law to look the other way. Why should I trust you?"

"Of course you shouldn't. I'm a criminal, just like you. But I am not without honor, and I can be a real asset to your organization. The way I've been for Lil' Miss Malachite."

Melanie harrumphed.

Parrot repeated the sound. "Indeed. The way you've been for Lil' Miss Malachite. Here you are, delivering her daughters to me."

"Well, to be honest they talk too much."

"Ugh," Melanie said.

"You're trying to play me like a fool," Parrot said.

"Play you like a fool?" Roman asked.

Parrot threw the crust of his toast at the wall. "Are you making fun of me?"

"No?" Roman said.

"No. Well then, who do you think I am? You want to trade for the Malachite girls? I offer you your life in exchange. Now go."

"But—"

"We already have the other girl, Torchwick. Found her snooping around behind the tavern, trying to sneak into the basement."

"What did you do to her?" Roman asked.

"I let her succeed."

Roman froze. "You're bluffing."

"*You're* bluffing. It's obvious that you care about her, which means you're up to something. I know what people say, that there's a treasure in a vault beneath my tavern. Well, that's true. But there's something else, too. Young Melanie is discovering my secret right now, and she will not survive."

"Miltia?" Melanie said.

"Miltia. Who cares?" Parrot calmly picked up another piece of toast.

Melanie and Roman locked eyes. They heard a girl scream from far away in the building.

Roman took off down the stairs. It wasn't until he reached the landing that he realized Badger hadn't even tried to stop him. In fact, none of the Parrots were standing in his way, and that worried him. But Miltia was downstairs and in trouble, and he had to save her—and her sister.

The door to the basement was locked. Well, he'd been wanting to give Melodic Cudgel a field test. He drew his cane and popped the reticle up. He aimed at the lock. He pulled the trigger.

A flare burst from the business end of the cane and destroyed the lock, along with half the door. He kicked the rest of it open and bolted down the stairs.

Miltia was standing in a corner of the basement facing off against a large, black *thing*.

The bony white spikes and glowing red streaks along its body marked it as a Creature of Grimm, the monstrous beasts that roamed Remnant, driven only to destroy humans and Faunus. But he'd never seen one like this before. It was like a rat or a mouse, only six times bigger and uglier. The long black tail whipping back and forth behind it had white barbs on its end, as vicious as its sharp, elongated claws.

Someone bumped into Roman from behind. He jumped. Melanie started to move forward but he grabbed her.

"Go upstairs," he whispered. "I'll take care of this. Whatever *this* is."

The monster's head snapped around to stare at Roman, its eyes blazing. It opened its mouth and hissed, revealing double rows of teeth as long as his fingers. "You were saying?" Melanie said.

"It's a Capivara Grimm." A screen on the wall turned on to show Paul Parrot's face. Roman noted the cameras positioned all around the room. He bet they were for more than security. Parrot liked to watch his victims die.

"I've never heard of anything like that in Mistral," Roman said.

"It's imported from the deserts of Menagerie. The Parrot syndicate has been . . . acquiring Capivara for a very long time."

"This is how you make your enemies disappear."

"This is how I make my enemies disappear." The door above them closed and Roman heard something heavy being dragged across the floorboards to block it.

"You wanted to see my treasure. Here it is." Parrot laughed.

"Keeping a Grimm in captivity is incredibly stupid and incredibly dangerous," Roman said.

Roman squeezed Melanie's hand reassuringly. He needed her and her sister to remain calm.

Roman had fought Grimm before. They sometimes got past the city guards and went on a rampage, especially in less protected settlements like Wind Path, where he had grown up. But when you faced death every day on the streets, the Grimm weren't so fearsome. At least it was a quicker death than freezing or starving.

Roman had fought Grimm before, but he had never killed one. Usually he held it off long enough for him to run away. But he'd seen plenty of Huntsmen and Huntresses take down Grimm. It didn't look that hard.

The first order of business was to get it away from Melanie and Miltia so they could escape.

"The back door," Roman whispered. "Look for your opening."

Melanie gave him a withering look. "Lil' Miss would be upset if she didn't get to kill you herself. We're staying to help."

"Okay. I tried," Roman said.

He moved in on the Capivara as Melanie and Miltia took up positions on either side of it. The Grimm twisted around, turning on each of them. It snapped at Roman and he smacked its snout with his cane. It lunged at him, razorblade claws lashing at his face, but he parried with his weapon and stepped to one side, firing a flare at one of its eyes point-blank. Black goo splattered from its ruined eye. It was angry now.

The Grimm leaped for Roman again, but it fell short. Melanie and Miltia were holding on to its tail. It scrabbled around, chasing the end of it—and them. They let go and cartwheeled to safety.

"It's pathetic," Roman said to Parrot. "You're pathetic. I really did respect you. I thought I wanted to be you. But I see that all of this—you didn't earn it."

"I didn't?"

"You inherited the Parrot syndicate from your uncle."

"I did kill him for it."

"And he inherited it from his father." Roman dodged another blow from the Grimm. He shot a flare at it and it backed up into the same corner it had trapped Miltia in moments ago. It snapped at him again, but Roman hooked his cane into its upper lip, like a fish on a line, turned, and flipped it overhead. The Capivara landed on its back and screeched.

"You didn't even capture this Grimm yourself," Roman said.

"How dare you!" Paul Parrot screamed. "How dare you! How dare you!"

"I think you broke him," Melanie said.

Roman fired a couple of times at the Grimm's tail before hitting it, severing its barbed tip. Even without it, it was still plenty deadly.

"You need to be more daring," Roman went on. "You aren't like Lil' Miss Malachite. She faced her fears; she earned the syndicate and made it her own—and her people love her for it. That's why we're loyal to her."

The Grimm hesitated. It looked at Roman, Melanie, and Miltia. Then it turned to look up the stairs. It sniffed.

"Why won't it kill you?" Parrot screamed.

Roman lowered his cane. "Grimm are drawn by emotion. You never controlled it. It killed your enemies because most people you drop in here are going to be afraid. They won't be able to fight back." Roman smiled at Melanie and Miltia. "But as far as I can tell, these girls don't feel *anything*. And I'm not afraid to die."

Melanie and Miltia rolled their eyes in tandem.

"Kill them!" Parrot shouted. "Kill them!"

The Capivara hissed once more at Roman, and then it ran up the stairs. It made short work of the barricade at the door. The men upstairs shouted. Roman heard Badger scream, and then the sound of a pool cue snapping in two. Then it was quiet.

"Anger can be a more powerful emotion than fear," Roman said. "Grimm's coming right for you, Paul."

When Roman looked at the screen next, Parrot was gone. He probably had an escape route—Roman would, in his place. But he hoped the Grimm would at least chase him for a bit and make him sweat.

"Did we just let a giant rat-mouse Grimm loose in the city?" Melanie asked.

"Eh. That's what Huntsmen and Huntresses are for. They'll handle it. And if it takes some of them out, that's just gravy."

He led them up the stairs. "Girls, you were terrific back there. All in a good day's work. Maybe we don't need to tell your mother about this, hmmm?"

"Uh-oh," Miltia said. At the top of the stairs, Spider reinforcements were waiting for them.

All things considered, an angry Lil' Miss Malachite was the scariest thing Roman had faced all day. She had him sit next to her, bowls of cottage cheese before them.

Roman eyed the lumpy white mess as he pushed berries around in it with a spoon.

"What is this supposed to be?" Roman said.

She put her spoon down, finished chewing, and dabbed at her mouth with a napkin. "Cottage cheese. Eat up."

"I know what's in the bowl, but I don't know what *this* is. Is it a reward? Is it a punishment?"

"You think I served you my favorite food as punishment."

"Well . . ."

"What do you think you deserve for that stunt you pulled, Torchwick?"

He glanced down at the bowl. He scrunched up his face. "I think it's a punishment."

"Maybe it is. Maybe knowing where you stand with me now is all the punishment you need."

She pushed her bowl away and turned to face him. With relief, he pushed his untouched bowl away, too, and looked at her.

"I trusted you. With my girls. And you offered them to one of my rivals."

"It was a ruse, and they agreed to it."

"They're teenagers."

"What were you doing when you were their age?"

One of her eyebrows lifted.

"Exactly. Don't underestimate them," he said.

"Never. However, you did almost get them killed by a Grimm. Which my crew then had to destroy."

"Thereby earning the Spiders some goodwill in the city! We took away Parrot's most valuable possession, what he used to make people afraid of him—*and* he was arrested! It all worked out." He paused. "Just like I planned."

Roman grabbed the spoon from his bowl and started to take a bite. Lil' Miss knocked it from his hand with her fan. Globs of cottage cheese splattered on Roman's face.

"And the fact that it somehow 'all worked out' is why you aren't dead, Torchwick."

He glanced at the cottage cheese nervously. Had she put poison in it?

"That isn't why I'm upset. I'm upset because you acted on your own instead of coming to me. You seem more interested in your own personal gain," Lil' Miss said.

"I only had your best interest in mind, ma'am. As always. I had to act swiftly to take advantage of the opportunity."

"I've already managed dear Chameleon," Lil' Miss said. "The only colors she'll be for a while are black and blue. Though if she hadn't told me where you went, the Spiders wouldn't have been there in time to save you."

"They didn't save us. They weren't even there!"

"Oh, they saved you. Because if you had tried to keep that massive screwup a secret, you would be wishing that Grimm had killed you. Consider this your last warning: Don't ever go behind my back again."

"Worried I'll see the knife you're hiding there?"

"When I kill you, Torchwick, you'll know it's coming." She reached over and wiped the cottage cheese off his cheek with a finger, almost like a caress.

Is she flirting? he suddenly wondered. He hadn't ever considered that she might like him, but if that was the case, he could use that to—

A sharp fingernail grazed the skin dangerously close to his right eye. "And death won't come from a knife."

She turned away from him and picked up her own spoon.

"Go on now. Get yourself cleaned up. With all this activity and the Parrots out of commission, there's a lull in the war. It's safe to come out from hiding—for now."

Roman stood and was surprised to feel how shaky his legs were. He was probably just tired. It had been a long day.

"Just to be clear. *I* wasn't hiding. The girls were hiding. I was just guarding them."

She stopped him before he left. "About that. Naturally I can't trust you to watch them again."

"I understand."

He held his grin in until he was back on the street.

Because of course that had been his true goal all along—a very calculated risk to demonstrate that when it came to babysitting, he was the wrong man for the job.

The last thing he wanted was to be responsible for some kid.

CHAPTER FIVE

HARD LESSONS

As Aurelia droned on about how Vale's attack on Mistrali settlers had started the Great War, Trivia let out an exaggerated yawn, patting at her mouth with her hand.

"Am I boring you?" her tutor asked.

Trivia closed her eyes and dipped her head forward until it touched her school Scroll. She startled "awake," jolting her hands to her sides and opening her eyes wide.

Aurelia laughed, despite herself. "History can be somewhat dry, but it's just as important as gymnastics."

But gymnastics is more fun, Trivia texted. What good will history ever be to me?

"It'll come in handy next week when I test you on everything we learn today."

Trivia twirled a finger over her head. Pass or fail, her parents would always be disappointed in her. There wasn't much motivation for her to do well—none of this mattered, and her performance only reflected on Aurelia's abilities as a teacher. It was her parents' fault for refusing to send Trivia to a real school, insisting that they could provide for her "special needs" better at home. But the real reason was that they wanted to be able to keep an eye on her.

She used to think they were embarrassed about her mismatched eyes and her muteness, and there *was* that, but she was starting to think there was another reason: They were worried about people finding out about what she could do.

And maybe they were afraid of what she would do.

"Whoopdee, indeed. However, your parents are investing quite a bit in your education. Not everyone can afford a combat school professor to tutor their child, and most of those who can never would think to."

Trivia raised an eyebrow. She texted a one-word message to her teacher's Scroll: Former.

Aurelia sighed. "That's right. Does that matter?"

Why did you give it up?

"I told you, I missed living in the city. That's all. Why are you bringing this up again?" She shook her head. "You're trying to distract me so you don't have to finish the day's lessons."

Trivia leaned back and smirked.

"What?" Aurelia asked. "What are you getting at?" She leaned forward.

Trivia shook her head. She lifted a hand to her lips, thumb and forefinger pressed together, pinkie out. She tipped her head up and pretended to sip, like she had when having imaginary tea parties with Neopolitan and her stuffed animals and action figures.

"Tea does sound nice." Aurelia put down her Scroll. "All right. Maybe it will wake you up. A little break and then we'll finish up the section with Vacuo's role in the war."

Trivia sighed.

"I'll be right back." Aurelia stood.

Trivia jumped up. She pointed to herself and then the door.

"You want to get the tea? All right. Just one sugar for me."

Trivia rushed out of the room. Neopolitan was waiting for her in the hall. She tossed up her hands. *Finally!*

Trivia held up a hand and moved her fingers and thumbs like a puppet's mouth. *Some people don't know when to shut up.*

They hurried toward the kitchen together. Trivia filled a kettle with water and placed it on the stove. While it heated up, she pulled out the bottle of sleeping pills Dr. Mazarin had prescribed for her, for her "nerves," and used a spoon to crush four of them. She swept the powder into a teacup just as the kettle whistled.

She dumped a bunch of tea leaves into the pot and swished it around impatiently. Neopolitan leaned her head on her arm on the counter and drummed her fingers.

Finally, it was ready. She piled the cups onto a tray, poured the tea, and added a sugar cube to Aurelia's. She stirred the sugar and the ground-up sleeping pills until they dissolved and added a splash of cream to her own cup, so there wouldn't be any chance of mixing them up.

Back in her room, she clinked glasses with Aurelia and watched her drink.

"It's a little more bitter than usual, isn't it?"

New blend from Mistral, Trivia texted. Very expensive.

"Of course it is. Well, back to work."

The sleeping pills worked quickly. Trivia only had to endure another three paragraphs before Aurelia nodded off, for real.

Neopolitan entered the room from the hall. Trivia flashed her a thumbs-up.

She dragged Aurelia over to her bed and tucked her in under the blanket, so her head was covered. Trivia pulled a printout from her desk drawer and left it on the table, then she grabbed the woman's purse and stepped into the hall. She heard footsteps approaching and thought quickly.

Her father was heading right toward her room.

"Leaving already? How did the lesson go today?" he asked.

Trivia extended a flat hand and tilted it back and forth. *So so.* She tried not to stare at her hand. Its skin was more brown than hers, and she liked the way Aurelia's silver ring caught the light.

She had been practicing with her Semblance, but it was still disorienting to be in another person's body, wearing their face and their clothes.

He grunted. "Trivia lacks motivation, but I know she's a smart girl. Maybe too smart for her own good. You'll let me know if she becomes a problem?"

Trivia nodded. Then she put a finger to her lips and pushed her hand down to her chest.

"Lower my voice?" he said more loudly.

Trivia tipped her head toward her bedroom door. She pressed her hands together and brought them up to rest her head on them like a pillow.

"Oh, she's sleeping. Why didn't you say so?" he said in a lower voice. "She does stay up until all hours. I'll see you out."

Trivia smiled and walked alongside him silently. He opened the door for her.

"Not that talkative today. I know how it is, when you have to do all the talking for both of you. But it seems like Trivia is rubbing off more on you than the opposite." He chuckled and shook his head. "See you on Thursday."

Trivia walked calmly toward Aurelia's car in the driveway. Neopolitan was waiting for her in the passenger seat. She clapped and grinned as Trivia took a seat.

We aren't out of here yet. Trivia looked at herself in the rearview mirror. Aurelia's green eyes looked back at her. She hadn't realized before how sad the woman looked. How tired she was.

She had some idea why. The research she had done on her teacher had turned up a story Aurelia would probably much rather forget. A student of hers had died on a training mission at Patch Combat School, lost in a scuffle with Ursa Grimm. The school didn't hold her responsible—she had managed to protect her fifteen other students, and it was all part of the risk. But there was plenty of blame to go around. The child's parents vowed to have her pay for the death of the girl, and Aurelia's official statement was, "I blame myself. She should still be with us. She was always so capable, perhaps I put too much faith in her to take care of herself while I got the others to safety."

The girl had been the same age as Trivia, only fifteen.

Aurelia had resigned soon after. But she hadn't done anything wrong in the eyes of the school, and her references had checked out, so Papa and Mama had no reason to suspect she was anything other than the perfect tutor for their daughter.

Neopolitan snapped her fingers. She pointed ahead of them.

Where are we going? Trivia looked down at the drab gray clothes

Aurelia favored. They weren't much more exciting than what Trivia wore—what her parents bought for her. She wished she could dress more like Neo, with her bright pink-and-white wardrobe.

So let's go shopping. Trivia put the key in the ignition and took a moment to familiarize herself with the controls. She had never driven a real car before, but she had played plenty of driving and flying simulation games.

The engine roared. She put her foot to the gas. The car rolled forward smoothly.

She grinned. Sometimes imitations were just as good as the real thing.

In a dressing stall at a Kaiser's department store, Trivia tried on another blouse, this one sky blue. She caught Neo's reflection in the mirror, gagging from behind her shoulder. Trivia blew her brown bangs away from her eyes and added the shirt to the growing discard pile.

The only shirt that met with Neo's approval was a pink pastel baby doll, which was more her style's than Trivia's. She flashed her a big thumbs-up and then pointed to white denim overalls on a hanger.

Really? Trivia thought. But she tried them on, and she had to admit they were cute. She undid her two long pigtails and shook her shoulder-length hair out. Neo clapped quietly.

Trivia tilted her head as she studied her reflection. Though she hadn't worn overalls since she was a little girl, wearing her hair down made her look older. She seemed more playful. Happier.

More like Neopolitan. No wonder her friend was so enthusiastic.

She added a pair of black combat boots and a black beaded necklace. She didn't look anything like herself.

It was perfect.

She felt a sense of loss when she activated her Semblance to project an illusion of the clothing she'd worn into the store over her fun new outfit. The fake clothes felt more constricting than the physical ones, which she kicked under the bench in the dressing stall. She even found it harder to breathe. Neo put a hand on her shoulder and another over her heart until she calmed down.

The real her was under the illusion, like it always was. It was just starting to hurt too much to hide it. That's why she'd had to leave her house today, leave Aurelia behind—if she didn't do something unexpected and different to break up her boring, predictable routine, she was going to lose touch with reality.

When she had calmed down, she stepped out of the stall. A young woman in a chic black-and-red dress, hair pinned up in an elegant do, approached and eyed her up and down.

"Didn't find anything you liked?"

Trivia shook her head.

"Would you like me to help? Maybe if you tell me what you're looking for. I'm sure we can find you something—"

Trivia's Scroll rang. She pulled it out. Papa was calling her.

She held up the phone and raised her eyebrows.

"Of course." The woman stepped aside and allowed Trivia to pass.

Trivia sent the call to voice mail and headed for the exit. When she stepped through the security scanners by the door, an alarm sounded. She tensed, ready to run.

But she stopped, turned, and put on an expression of puzzled annoyance.

"Sorry, miss. I'm sure there's something wrong with them, but would you mind waiting just a moment?" A brawny security guard stepped over to her.

Trivia shrugged.

She was disguising the stolen clothes, but they still had the store's tags on them, with their anti-theft devices. Next time she'd have to remember to remove those.

Of course there was going to be a next time.

Then she saw the saleslady come running out of the dressing room at the far end of the shop, holding two empty hangers in one hand, waving Trivia's drab brown skirt in the other. The same as the one Trivia appeared to still be wearing.

"Stop her!" the woman shouted.

Trivia's heart started racing and she knew she had dropped the illusion for just a moment because the guard stepped back and said, "What the?" He recovered and reached for his holstered gun.

Trivia wiggled her fingers good-bye and somersaulted backward, kicking her legs up and just grazing the man's chin with a boot-clad foot. She came up facing the other direction and glimpsed Neo holding up a sign: 9.5.

Some friend you are, she thought.

She kicked the doors open and ran.

Trivia didn't return home until late. There wasn't much point in going back sooner. Her father's text messages made it quite clear that they had discovered Aurelia and knew she was gone. Neo convinced her she should enjoy herself while she could because she might not have another chance for a while.

By the time she drove up to the mansion, the car was full of things she had stolen from shops all over the city of Vale. Three pairs of boots, a dozen tops, seven jackets, three skirts. All in bright colors that didn't match anything in her wardrobe. She skipped up to the front door wearing the last outfit she had shoplifted, a white ball gown with a pink lace trim and belt sash. Hooked on her forearm was a closed white-and-pink paper parasol.

She opened the door and paused on the threshold, listening. The house was dark, but it was unsettling because she had expected more commotion. Police waiting to talk with her, perhaps. Her parents greeting her with stony faces at the entryway. She figured at the very least they would have waited up for her.

But the house was quiet. She checked her Scroll. The last message from her father had been more than two hours ago. Just two words: "We're worried."

Trivia walked through the house tentatively. She finally heard her father's voice coming from his study. He was still up, working probably. Trivia approached the open door. He was leaning wearily over his desk talking to someone on-screen.

"Thank you. Consider your debt repaid, Chief." He disconnected the call and leaned back in his chair with a heavy sigh, eyes closed.

Trivia stepped back, but her paper parasol brushed against the doorframe roughly. Papa bolted up in his seat. He spotted her.

"Oh, it's you. Feeling any better?"

Trivia stepped into the room and pressed a hand against her forehead. Her mother got a lot of migraines. She claimed they were because of Trivia.

"Go back to bed, Carmel. I know you're worried, but right now you need your sleep. I'll deal with her when she comes home."

Trivia nodded. She smiled, in the slightly sad way her mother often did. It was so easy to mimic other people. It wasn't just the face and the clothes, it was all the little mannerisms that they probably didn't even know about. The little tells that betrayed what they were thinking, even when their mouths said something else. Those were the details that made most people terrible liars.

Papa's chair creaked as he stood. Jimmy Vanille came closer and studied the face of the person he thought was his wife. "You look exhausted."

Trivia tipped her head in acknowledgment. That was kind of a rude thing to say to someone, but that was Papa: He said whatever he was thinking. That's where Trivia got it from, except not so much with the saying part.

"Probably because you've had such a busy day. Trivia." He snapped his fingers and the door to the study slammed shut behind her. She jumped. "No more running, kid."

Trivia glared at him. *How did you know?*

"You're wondering how I figured it out? If you want to know whether someone is lying to you, it's all in their eyes."

Trivia turned to look at herself in the mirror over the credenza. One eye was brown like her mother's, the other was pink. She had been pushing her Semblance all day, and she was tired—too tired to maintain her mother's appearance for long.

"Besides, I know my wife well enough to tell when it's not her—if only because she is uncharacteristically quiet. And I know my daughter. That's enough, Trivia. Please, no more charades."

She let go of the illusion and put her hands on her hips. *Charades?*

"Poor choice of words. But thank you, that's much better. You are never to impersonate your mother or me again. In fact, you are not to use your Semblance in this house ever again—preferably at all."

He sat down at his desk and steepled his fingers. "What *are* you wearing?"

Trivia spun around in her gown and then curtsied. *Do you like it?*

"You've been on quite a tear today. I don't know what you were thinking. Drugging your teacher? Really, Trivia?"

Trivia cupped her hand and mimed taking a swig from a bottle.

"She does not have a drinking problem. Her tea was laced with sleeping powder. Her only mistake was trusting you. A mistake we've all made at one time or another."

Trivia crossed her arms.

"Right. And there was the little matter of her record. I found the article in your room, which I'm sure you hoped I would. Did you think that would excuse your actions? Did you think I wasn't aware of what happened to that student at Patch? That's why I hired Aurelia. I wanted someone who knows how to handle a child with an untrained Semblance, someone who couldn't be hired anywhere else. It's much easier that way to buy their silence."

Trivia stuck her tongue out.

"You know what I mean. Regardless, she won't be coming back here."

Trivia widened her eyes.

"Don't act all shocked and innocent. I didn't fire her. She quit. I gave her a generous severance package to avoid any uncomfortable conversations with the law, as well as one of our cars." He shook his head. "Though I would have fired her. She may have underestimated her student's abilities, costing her life, but it can be just as bad to underestimate what someone is capable of. And if she ever breathes a word about this family to anyone, she won't get off so easy."

He leaned forward and rested his arms on his desk. "Speaking of getting off easy. What was the point of your crime spree all over town?"

Trivia scratched her head.

"You don't know? The only reason you aren't in jail right now is because I convinced all those businesses not to press charges. I try to keep our family out of the public eye, but today you threw all that away. I had everyone on the alert for you, and I knew exactly where you were and what you stole."

Trivia frowned. Could he be telling the truth?

"Why did you feel the need to take those things? We give you everything you need. Everything you ask for."

Trivia held up the parasol.

"We have plenty of umbrellas, Trivia."

But I wanted this one, she thought. *I wanted something of my own that didn't come from you. I wanted to see what I could do on my own for once.*

"If you're ever going to speak up for yourself, now's the time," he said.

She groaned and reached for her Scroll.

"Don't bother. I don't want to *read* another of your excuses. I want to hear my daughter's voice for the first time. Say something, anything, and all is forgiven. We'll make this right, kid."

She looked down at the floor. She twisted the tip of the parasol into the lush green carpeting.

"All right. We'll talk about this more tomorrow. I've had enough of you for one day." He slumped back in his chair. "I've already paid for everything you took, double what it was all worth. And you will be donating all of the stolen items to charities."

Trivia ground the parasol tip deeper into the carpet. Just like that, he had taken away the best day of her life. She had thought she was being cunning and powerful, but daddy had paid everyone off to look the other way. The things she had claimed for herself were just more stuff her parents had paid for.

She drew the parasol back and hurled it at her father. It flew straight and fast, like a spear, and the tip struck him in the face, knocking him and his chair backward. He bellowed as they toppled to the floor.

He pulled himself up. He had a cut over his right eyebrow. A couple of inches lower and she would have struck him in the eye. He touched the wound delicately and winced, examining the blood on his fingers.

She should have felt bad, she supposed, guilty for hurting him, but she didn't feel anything.

He gaped at her in shock. "Trivia! What has gotten into you?"

No, she did feel something after all. Satisfaction.

She had done something unexpected, uncharacteristic—surprising even herself. And unlike everything she had done today, that act couldn't be erased. She had done something that had made a real impact.

She walked slowly toward her father. He held his ground, waiting for a sign of apology. Was she imagining it, or did he seem wary of her?

She walked past him, bent down, and picked up her parasol. She examined it carefully for damage.

He reached out toward her, but stopped short of placing his hand on her shoulder. "What's wrong with you? What do you want?" he whispered.

She glared at him. *I want you to leave me alone. I want to be far away from here.*

He clenched his hand into a fist. "Get out! Go to your room!"

She opened the parasol, turned, and strolled toward the door, twirling it behind her on her shoulder. She jiggled the knob, but it was locked.

She snapped her fingers the way her father had. The door unlatched and opened. Papa growled.

Neopolitan was outside his office waiting for her, as always. Her friend clapped a hand to her eye and took a pratfall backward dramatically. She popped back up, mouth open in soundless laughter.

Trivia smiled. That *had* been pretty funny. In fact, right now she was in a brighter mood again.

Today had been the perfect day.

CHAPTER SIX

CHEAT

As Roman approached Broken Memories, swinging his cane and whistling a jaunty tune, the shop's lights went dark and the neon OPEN sign fizzled out.

Roman reached the shop door and jiggled the knob. Locked. He tapped gently on the glass with his cane and waited.

"Bisque, I know you're in there. Your hours are posted right here, and it's still an hour before closing."

He saw a figure shift behind the counter at the back of the store. "I had to close early today! Something came up!"

Other figures moved around. Roman peered through the glass. A Scroll lit up in the darkness. He heard a sharp, "Switch that off!" before the screen went out.

"You still have customers inside. Come on, Bisque. I'm just picking up what you owe me."

Roman tapped again on the glass. Harder. *WHAM.* The glass cracked. He hit it again—harder. *WHAM.* The crack spider-webbed throughout the reinforced pane.

"Now." *WHAM.* "Look." *WHAM.* "What." *WHAM.* "You." *WHAM.* "Made." *WHAM.* "Me." *WHAM.* "Do."

The glass shattered and small gems of glass cascaded down. Someone screamed.

Roman stepped through and flipped the light switch. "Looks like you're still open after all! Guess we'll see if you can really fix anything." He whipped out his cane and knocked a computer screen off the workbench, sending it crashing to the floor.

"In my experience, some things are harder to mend than others, and the healing process can be long and painful." Roman looked at the customers huddling on the floor behind a display of Scroll-charging cables. One of them, a pimpled boy with messy brown hair, was holding his Scroll up, recording video of Roman.

Roman sighed and pointed his cane at the boy. "Drop it, hero."

"N-no!" The boy stood up, still holding his Scroll up in his shaky hands.

Roman waited a beat and then he activated the targeting reticule on his cane. It took the kid a second to realize what it meant.

"Three . . . two . . . ," Roman counted.

The boy dropped the Scroll with a yelp.

Roman shot the Scroll just before it hit the floor. It flipped up into the air, the holographic screen blinking out. The boy fumbled and caught it. The electronics sizzled and popped as it died, releasing a tendril of gray smoke.

"That Scroll, for instance. Pretty sure it's dead." Roman squinted his right eye and aimed at the broken Scroll in the boy's hand, which lined up dangerously close with the boy's heart. "No bringing that back to life."

"Enough!" Bisque said. "These are my customers. Please! Let them go."

"Of course!" He lowered his cane and gestured with it toward the door. "Thank you for your business. Please come again."

The four customers hesitated for a moment, but then the boy with the broken Scroll went for the door. When the others saw he had made it out, they followed suit.

"Four customers. Glad to see business is booming." He aimed at a shelf of repaired electronics and fired his weapon. An old video game console exploded.

"No thanks to you. Please stop! These things aren't cheap to replace."

Bisque loved machines more than he did people, and he seemed able to coax almost any broken device back to working order, no matter how far gone. That was just a cover of course; his real business was reverse-engineering the latest Atlas tech and cloning it for the black market. He was highly skilled and highly sought after— both from people who wanted to hire him, and the police who wanted to arrest him.

"Speaking of cheap." Roman strode toward the frazzled technician. "Lil' Miss and the Spiders devote considerable resources toward keeping you up and running. But when I come to collect our fee, you try to hide? You can't escape us any more than an insect caught in a web can free itself. You're just stuck."

Roman hooked his cane through the short man's suspenders. He wasn't going anywhere.

"I can't keep paying these higher rates, Mr. Torchwick. Monthly payments were bad enough. I was just getting by. But double that is going to do me in."

"You're a savvy businessman. What's the cost of *not* paying?"

Bisque placed his hands on the counter and leaned forward. "If I could just speak to Lil' Miss Malachite, I'm sure we could work out a deal."

"You speak to me, and I speak to Lil' Miss. *This* is the deal." Roman smacked the cane down on the counter, half an inch from Bisque's fingers. The man jumped back and cradled his hands to his chest.

"Careful! My hands are worth more than you'll ever be."

Roman froze. "So that's it. You think you're better than me. Because you went to school? Learned a trade?"

Bisque's eyes widened. "No. No, I didn't say that!"

"Maybe I'm too stupid to read between the lines."

Bisque shook his head. "No! I misspoke."

Roman walked around the shop, his cane out and dragging the devices on the shelves to the floor. He left a trail of broken Scrolls, toy robots, cameras, clocks, and other junk.

When he had made it all around the room and back to Bisque, pale and quivering, Roman smiled.

"All right. You want to make a new deal? Here's my best offer. Left or right?"

"What does that mean?"

Roman lifted his eyes skyward. "It isn't hard. Choose one: Left or right?"

"But what am I choosing from?"

"That would be telling."

"L-left?"

"And we have a deal!" Roman grabbed Bisque by both suspenders and lifted him up and over the counter. He turned and slammed the little man down onto his back on his workbench.

"Now don't move, or I might miss." Roman stepped back and lifted his cane over his head.

Bisque held up his hands. "Please, don't!"

"You think I enjoy this, Bisque?" *It's only my favorite part of the job*, he thought. Crime doesn't pay, especially when you work for Lil' Miss. But he could at least have some fun with it. "Just give me what you owe and I'll leave."

"I can't, Mr. Torchwick! I don't have the money. But I'll pay you extra next time, I promise."

"Look at this place. You aren't going to have enough to pay me next time, either. You're probably planning on skipping town. But that's going to be harder with a broken leg, I think."

Bisque squeaked.

"Left, did you say?" Roman lifted his cane again and prepared to smash in the man's left knee.

"That's enough, Roman." Chameleon stepped into the store, her skin shifting to its normal bronze—except for the left side of her face, which vanished into the colors behind her to hide the scars crisscrossing her cheek. She didn't wear much clothing these days, both because it thwarted her natural camouflaging abilities, and because when she chose to show herself, it could be quite distracting.

"Cammie. You're getting much better at the camouflage thing." No wonder she had fallen back into Lil' Miss's favor. Her Semblance had value in her work, when she could hide herself in plain sight and overhear all sorts of information. "How long have you been standing there?"

"Too long," she said. "Let him go."

"Hey, I don't interrupt you while you're working."

"This isn't your job, Roman. I know you've been doing a little side hustle." She tilted her head.

Roman stepped back, drawing his cane behind his back.

"Does Lil' Miss know?" he asked.

"What do you think? She knows all . . . eventually. You've been collecting double payments from businesses, for a while now."

"Who figured it out?"

She put a hand on her hip. "That would be telling."

"So I guess I'm fired."

"No one gets fired. Spiders are in the family for life. When they get out of line, they get squished."

Roman nodded. "I knew this day would come. But I hoped it wouldn't be you."

"I requested this assignment." She crossed her arms. "I finally realized I was just a side thing, too."

"Don't flatter yourself." He laughed. "I know hiding is kind of your whole thing, but it sure looks like you came here unarmed."

Her skin flashed crimson. "That's not why, you idiot." She scowled. "I wanted to understand. I thought you were happy. Why aren't— Aren't we good enough for you?"

"I've never been happy, and I expect I never will. But that doesn't mean I'm going to try to stop buying happiness."

Roman walked around her, stepping sideways, to keep her in his sights—and maneuver himself closer to the door. It wasn't that he didn't think he could beat her. He figured there would be others on the way. If they weren't already waiting for him. He resisted the urge to glance out the window. You did not want to take your eyes off Cammie.

Her skin crept closer toward purple. "Do you even know what you want, Roman?"

He spread his arms. "I want more. I want everything! I want people to know my name."

"You've got that," she said. "There's already a bounty on your head, and everyone in Mistral, crooks and Huntsmen alike, are going to be looking for you."

Something was up. She didn't have to tell him that. Oversharing wasn't in her nature, and she wasn't one to put off a fight.

"I'm impressed Lil' Miss is putting big money on this," Roman said. "She didn't get where she is by spending frivolously."

"She has to. It's the only way she can separate herself from the scheming and double-dealing you did in her name. You haven't just lost her protection. She . . ." Cammie sighed. "She needs you gone for good."

Roman tilted his head, considering. She was being very particular with her words, unless he was imagining it. And she still wasn't trying to hit him. He didn't know if he should dare to read into any of that.

Then she disappeared as she took on the colors and shading of her background. She really had gotten better at that. But, like everyone, she had a tell.

Roman glimpsed a subtle shimmering on his right, like heat radiating from pavement on a summer day. He spun and lashed out with his cane, blocking Cammie's roundhouse kick. Her clothes were made out of some fancy new material that adapted to light, the result of Atlesian experiments with cloaking technology—with actual cloaks. In a rare crime deal some years back, she had shared her intel about a secret transport from Argus with Lemon, a crime lord in Kuchinashi. In exchange, she had run the operation to hijack it. And in true form, Lil' Miss has gotten away with the entire shipment.

Invisibility cloaks were a hot commodity in the Mistral underworld, especially for a network of spies. And her own tech geniuses had figured out how to make the material adapt to Cammie's Semblance.

Lil' Miss took care of her own, he'd give her that, he thought wistfully. And she was just as fastidious about making sure that those who crossed her got what they deserved.

Roman blindly blocked Cammie's flurry of attacks, relying on his senses to detect her mainly by hearing and anticipating her movements. When she moved fast, sometimes her skin and her invisible clothes lagged behind a bit, causing the background to tear and stutter. Not everyone would know to look for that or be able to react quickly enough, anticipating where she would be instead of striking where she had been.

It was mostly instinct, and Roman had honed good instincts during his time in the organization. It was a bit of luck.

It also helped that he and Cammie had sparred with each other quite a bit over the years. He had probably trained more with her than he had anyone else in the gang.

"You're holding back," Roman said.

"I'm just toying with you," she said. "You should know the difference. I learned it from you."

So she was trying to slow him down. For what?

He ducked and felt her fist whiff by his head, nearly knocking off his hat. He swept his cane out low. When he felt it make contact, he twisted to hook her ankle and he pulled. She slammed down hard and for a moment a rainbow rippled across her skin from the impact. He fired at her. She rolled out of the way just in time and disappeared again.

He looked around, but he couldn't see her telltale shimmer anymore. Either she had stripped for added stealth—it wouldn't be the first time—or . . .

He looked up. One of the bare fixtures dangling on a long cable from the ceiling swayed slightly.

"I've learned some things from you, too." Roman shot at the light. The bulb exploded and glass tinkled down. A moment later, Cammie reappeared—in the process of flying toward him. She hit Roman headfirst and pushed him backward. She held tight to his lapel, so that as her momentum carried her in a backflip over his head, she pulled him along with her and flipped him over her head.

Roman soared across the shop and landed in a pile of broken computers with a jarring crunch. The air went out of him.

"Cute." He wheezed.

"You aren't bad yourself." Her skin took on a rosy tint. "Except for that ponytail."

"What's wrong with my—" He blinked and she was gone.

Two could play at that game. Roman raised the reticule on his cane and aimed carefully, panning around the room. Something shimmered in the corner of his eye, but he ignored it until he found his true target.

He fired at the light switch by the door and the room plunged into darkness, lit only with dim bands of light from the streetlamps outside seeping through the slats of the window blinds.

"You always did like the shadows," Cammie said. "People say I have a lot to hide, but you have more secrets than anyone."

"Secrets are deadly, but the truth kills."

Roman fired randomly around the room, the resulting fireworks briefly filling it with a red glow. Something caught fire.

The adaptive tech on Cammie's clothing took a moment to adjust with the sudden shift in illumination, and tiny shards of the broken bulb twinkled in the flickering light of the flames.

Roman kept her in his sights as he continued to fire, scoring three out of five hits on her. The last one broke her Aura and she faded back into view as she stumbled, fell, and skidded to a halt. Roman approached her prone form and rolled her onto her back with his foot.

She glared at him.

"Still glad you came to kill me?" Roman asked.

Her face relaxed. "You idiot."

"Excuse me? That's an odd choice for your last words."

"I didn't come here to kill you. I came to say good-bye." She rolled her head in the direction of the door. Spotlights were shining on the front of the store, and Roman saw silhouettes slowly moving in. "*They're* here to kill you, in case I failed."

Roman stared at her in disbelief.

"Why?" he asked.

"Because we might have made good partners once."

"I work better alone."

"That wouldn't be my takeaway from this situation." She coughed. Maybe from her injuries, maybe from the smoke starting to fill the room. "Consider that you might have gotten what you wanted after all if you hadn't been in it only for yourself. If you had allowed yourself to trust someone."

"Life doesn't work that way. Not mine, anyway."

The only person Roman had ever trusted, his mother, had left him in a children's orphanage in Wind Path. That had taught him an important lesson that he would never forget.

Lie. Cheat. Survive.

And maybe it was time to work on that last part.

"Go on. You have to do it," Cammie said.

Roman lifted his cane over his head.

"Bye, Roman." She closed her eyes just before he whacked her. She was knocked out cold.

Better that way for her, he thought, as he snuck out the back door. He heard shouting from inside the shop. Sirens from the fire brigade. He'd made a mess of things, just the way he liked to.

He took one of the longer twisting routes back to his old hideaway. He had to get out of the city, but he needed two things first: a change of clothes, because these were all sooty and smoky, and the money he'd packed away over the years—his very small cut of jobs done for Lil' Miss, the spoils of some of his side jobs, and the more sizable funds he'd been collecting for six months as part of his unsanctioned extortion.

He slid aside the secret panel above the window and reached in. Empty.

He slammed his fist against the wall. He'd been so careful, but someone had found his hideout and stolen from him. It was probably the same someone who had ratted him out. So much for honor among thieves. They could have at least given him the chance to pay them off for their silence.

Whoever it was must have had something to gain by eliminating Roman. Or a bone to pick with him. He could obviously rule out Chameleon, begrudgingly. But when he found out who it was—

He smashed his cane into his table, cracking it in two. He took a deep breath. He reached back into the hidden compartment and pushed up gently, releasing a second hiding spot. A tight roll of Lien dropped into his hand.

They had taken a lot from him, but not all of it. It wasn't much, but it was enough for a fresh start. But where?

Nowhere in Mistral would be safe for him with a hit out on him. In fact, if Lil' Miss really wanted him dead, nowhere in Remnant would be safe.

Vacuo was a good place to hide, but the desert was probably one of the few fates worse than Lil' Miss. And while there was a thriving criminal element, it wouldn't be particularly welcoming to a newcomer. There was no future for Roman there.

Atlas?

Roman laughed to himself. Mantle offered slim pickings for criminals like himself. The crime syndicates ran on Atlas money, so it was hard to make a dent on your own. Plus, the price of getting caught was too high. Solitas was also a little too frigid for a fair-weather guy like him.

So Vacuo was too hot; Atlas was too cold—that left Vale. Plenty of territory, lots of opportunity to carve out a niche in the capital city, and those crime bosses had never seen anyone like Roman Torchwick before. As an added bonus, Lil' Miss had made plenty of enemies in Vale, which made the insider knowledge Roman had of her operations extremely valuable.

He'd be running the show there in less than a year.

CHAPTER SEVEN

FALLING OUT

Trivia knelt before her bedroom door, probing the lock with a tension wrench and pick rake she'd fashioned from a hairpin. She just couldn't get this one to open. She consulted the tutorial video "How to Pick Any Lock" on her Scroll once more, and repeated the motions exactly.

She applied gentle pressure to the tension wrench, so it would rotate the plug slightly. Then she scraped the pick against the binding pins. She felt some of them slide up and lock into place above the shear line, but she just couldn't get one of them to budge. She tried to hold everything in place while she reached for another pick, but the slight movement caused the pick to slip and all the pins fell back down.

No! She had almost had it!

She threw the picks across the room, narrowly missing Neopolitan. Her friend was wearing a brown duster over a rose-pink corset and black tights, something Trivia had seen online and thought might make a fun outfit. It suited Neo, at least.

Neo scooped up the picks and held them up, a smirk on her face.

Trivia gestured at the first three locks that she had managed to unlock, though they had taken her most of the night. Over the last few months, the locks on her door had been increasing in complexity; in the process, she was becoming quite the lock pick. But this last one was just too tricky and too new. She hadn't even been able to find any diagrams or guides on cracking it yet.

Papa had promised that if this didn't keep her in, he'd upgrade to a hard light force field, joking that the Altesian tech would be cheaper than putting their local locksmith's children through Beacon.

Neo's face lit up and Trivia groaned to herself. That always meant that her friend had come up with an idea that was likely to get Trivia in trouble. An idea she just couldn't say no to, because it was also too much fun to pass up.

Neo dropped the lock picks and pointed at a can of hair spray on Trivia's makeup table.

Hair spray? Trivia picked it up. She shot Neo a questioning look.

Neo swept a hand toward Trivia's night table, which held a book of fairy tales, a hand bell, and a chocolate-scented candle. Trivia guessed and held up the candle.

She studied the two objects in her hand for a moment before she realized what Neo had in mind. She looked up at the girl.

Neo winked.

Trivia lit the candle and wondered how much heat it would take to melt it. She shook the can of hair spray. Did she have enough?

Even if it didn't melt the lock, the heat would cause the metal to expand slightly, which might make it easier to coax the tumblers into place.

Here goes. Trivia held the burning candle in front of the lock and pressed her index finger against the little button on top of the can, aiming the nozzle at the small flame.

She pushed a little harder, wincing in anticipation.

Neo clapped and Trivia pushed down hard, spraying a fine chemical mist toward the candle.

WHOOSH!

The small flame burst into a plume of fire. Trivia felt the heat on her face. She leaned back and held the makeshift flamethrower steady on the lock. The shiny brass turned black and the paint around it blistered and bubbled. It smelled like melting crayons.

And then the door caught fire.

Trivia gasped and dropped the candle and can. She stomped on the candle to stamp out the flame, but fire continued to envelop the door, smaller, bright blue flames dripping from it onto the carpet.

Neo stepped up to the door and knocked gently on it. She looked at Trivia, her mouth a small O.

The door is made of wood.

Trivia grabbed a pillow and started beating at the fire, but all she did was set the pillow on fire. She tossed it on the ground and kicked it. It burst into a cloud of burning feathers. She rolled her eyes and backed away. The room was filling with smoke, and the fire was spreading rapidly.

Trivia couldn't call for help of course. She looked down at where she had left her Scroll, on the floor by the door, which was already consumed in fire. So she also couldn't *text* for help either.

Do something! Trivia glared at Neopolitan. Neo crouched down and warmed her hands over the spreading flames, rubbing them together.

Trivia looked around her room for something that she could use to put out the fire. Why wasn't there an extinguisher in here?

All she saw were copious amounts of stuff that would feed the fire: books, board games, clothes. Useless junk that her parents had kept giving her, thinking they could buy her love or make her room seem less like a prison. Stuff that she had fantasized about burning in a bonfire to show them how little she cared for it all.

She coughed and blinked. It was getting hard to see now.

Maybe it hadn't been such a good idea to start a fire in a locked room. The damn door was probably going to burn down before the lock melted.

She could have used her hair dryer to heat up the lock instead, she realized now.

She retreated deeper into her suite, but without inner doors to close, she was just buying herself a little time. The smoke was probably going to get her before the fire would.

In the distance, a smoke alarm went off. But Trivia was home alone for the evening. Her parents had gone out and locked her into her room to prevent her from getting into more trouble.

Trivia laughed, but her throat was so raw it came out as a wheezing cough.

She had to open a window.

In the back of her mind, she realized that opening a window would only feed the fire, pulling it through the room more quickly. But if she didn't get air, she would die.

The window stuck at first. She shoved until it swung open. She leaned out of it, sucking in fresh, cool air. Smoke billowed around her, spilling into the night. Their house was miles from anyone, but she hoped someone would see the smoke in time.

She felt a wall of heat pushing against her back. She looked down. Her room was on the top floor, at the back of the house, about forty feet above the ground. Too far to jump, even if she rolled like she had learned in gymnastics. But her Aura should give her some protection. If only she had something to slow her fall.

She ducked back into the room. She couldn't see anything now, but she felt her way to her bed and reached under it. She fumbled around, grasping, until her hand closed on the handle of the parasol she had stolen three years before. The one she had used to strike Papa.

She ran back toward the window and leaped, before she could change her mind.

She flew out and away from the burning room and immediately felt relief from the raging inferno. She wasn't burning anymore, but now she was plunging downward.

She held the parasol up, grabbed on to it with both hands, and pressed the button to open it.

It flew open and she was yanked up and back as the paper canopy caught the air. She dangled as she drifted down toward the sprawling garden. She had seen this in a movie once, but she couldn't believe it was actually working.

As she drifted down, she felt like Alyx falling through the world. Then she heard a tearing sound. She looked up and noticed the constellation of scorch marks in the paper as the wind and gravity began to rip it apart. She concentrated and patched it up with her Semblance, reinforcing the fragile paper, imagining it as a thin, light, durable film that absolutely would not shred and drop her twenty feet to the ground.

She drifted lower, but so did her Aura—already drained from protecting her from the heat of the fire for so long. She looked down past her kicking legs. Fifteen feet, maybe. She had a choice. Hold the umbrella together for as long as possible, risking a bad fall, or releasing her physical illusion and hoping she had enough Aura left to cushion her landing.

She let go of the illusion and the parasol in the same moment and plummeted, eyes squeezed shut. To her surprise and relief, someone caught her before she hit the ground. She opened her eyes and Neopolitan smirked before her form glitched and Trivia dropped through her briefly insubstantial arms to the ground. Neo covered her mouth in a silent laugh.

Trivia was on the verge of exhaustion, but she kept burning the last of her Aura to hold Neo together. To hold herself together.

Trivia sat at the entrance to the garden, arms wrapped around her knees. Neo curled beside her with an arm over her shoulder. They watched the top floor of the Vanille mansion as it was consumed by flames.

It's so pretty, she thought.

She heard sirens in the distance at the same time a car roared up the driveway. Her mother shouted at the front of the house, calling for her.

Trivia and Neo waited until Mama and Papa found them. Her parents pointedly ignored Neo, as they always did when she appeared in their presence.

"Thank the Brothers you're all right!" Mama said.

Papa seemed more concerned about the house than Trivia. He gazed up at the fire eating away at the top floor. A section of roof caved in where Trivia's room had been. He flinched.

"What have you done?" Papa roared. He rushed toward Trivia and grabbed her by the shoulders, pulling her to her feet. "You stupid girl!"

"Jimmy!" Mama grabbed his arm. "It's all right. We can fix the damage."

He shoved her off him, but he let go of Trivia. Her arms stung where he had squeezed them with a clawlike grip. Papa turned away from both of them and resumed watching the window of her room, as if he was expecting something to happen.

Trivia stepped back, appalled. Papa had yelled at her, punished her, even ignored her over the years, but he had never hurt her before.

Trivia looked to her mother for help. She was flustered and confused. "Jimmy, what is it? What are you looking for?"

"She could have blown us all up," he muttered. "And now the fire department will be in there, and who knows what they'll—" He shook his head. "Cops too. They'll want to search the house." He glanced at his wife. "We could be ruined."

"I don't understand. What are you worried about? At least we're all safe."

"Forget it," he said. "Better if you don't know."

"It was just an accident." She looked at Trivia. Her voice hardened. "It *was* just an accident?"

Trivia nodded.

"I can't imagine *what* were you thinking, Trivia."

Trivia shrugged. She pointed at Neo, who smiled and flipped her hair back. She held the singed and torn parasol over her right shoulder.

"No!" Papa said. "This is all *your* fault, Trivia!"

"I'm so tired of 'Neo this' and 'Neo that'!" Mama stalked toward the pink-haired girl. "She. Isn't. Real."

She drew her right hand back and slapped Neo. The girl shattered into hundreds of small pink shards. Trivia rushed forward and tried to gather the pieces back together but they fell through her fingers. The last of her Aura fizzled out and Trivia collapsed to her knees as the broken fragments of her only friend swirled around her like flower petals in the wind . . . and faded.

The approaching sirens grew louder. Trivia stared at the empty space where her friend had been, tears streaming down her face. She had felt a shift inside her at the moment Neo had vanished— like her heart had broken, or something had been set free.

Even an imaginary friend is better than no friend at all, and Neo had been so much more to Trivia. Now she was gone.

I'm right where I've always been, said a voice in Trivia's head. The only voice Trivia had was her internal monologue, the one that said things she couldn't say aloud. Neopolitan had always been that other voice who told her what to do, who comforted her when she was sad and alone, who always knew what she was thinking and what she truly wanted deep down.

Dr. Mazarin had often talked to Trivia about Neo, trying to make her understand that her imaginary friend was very real—to her—but that she was also a part of her. Unlike Papa and Mama,

Dr. Mazarin hadn't wanted Trivia to send her away or pretend she didn't exist. She had said Neo would leave one day when Trivia was ready. When she wasn't needed anymore.

Oh, I'm not going anywhere, Neo said. *Just try to get rid of me.*

She sounded like Trivia. She had always looked like Trivia too, the way she wished she could be. Neopolitan represented everything Trivia didn't have: the freedom to express herself. The carefree spirit to do whatever she wanted.

Trivia smiled. She took in a deep breath. She felt complete for the first time.

She felt like herself.

Get up.

Trivia hopped lightly to her feet. She thought she would be shaky and weak, but she had flawless balance. She felt strong.

"I never want to see that thing again," Papa said. "Do you hear me?!"

Trivia pretended to wince and covered her ears. She rolled her eyes. *Obviously. I'm mute, not deaf.*

Papa glared at her in astonishment. She hadn't said a word, but she had clearly communicated her disdain.

He stomped toward her and raised a hand to hit her. "You little—"

"Jimmy!" Mama said.

Trivia put her hands on her hips and locked eyes with him. She raised an eyebrow and smiled, daring him to touch her.

He scowled and walked away. She heard one of his cars start and drive off, before the sirens and heavy boots on gravel drowned out the sound.

"It's clear that you don't want to be a part of this family anymore. Maybe you never did," her mother said. "You would rather burn it to the ground than stay here."

Trivia licked her lips. Without her Scroll, her communication boards, she couldn't respond. If she could even find the words for what she was feeling.

"So be it," her mother went on.

Trivia grabbed her mother's arm, but Mama shrugged her off.

"We can't do anything more for you. We don't know what you need. But there's one place that might be able to help. Train you to be a better person." She stroked Trivia's cheek and brushed a lock of hair from her pink eye. She seemed surprised by what she saw in her daughter's face. "Help you become a whole person."

Trivia's heart raced. *They're sending me away? Where?*

That's all Trivia had ever wanted, to be someplace where she fit in. Where she could be herself. Where she didn't have to listen to her parents or hide what she could do.

"Maybe you'll even make some friends. Real ones. And learn how to control yourself. Get a handle on your . . ." She waved her hand in the air, to indicate Trivia's Semblance.

The hope Trivia had felt died. Her mother wasn't offering her freedom. She was just sending her to a different prison.

"At least you won't have much to pack." Her mother laughed harshly. She nodded absently and then left to talk to the firefighters, leaving Trivia alone by the garden with smoke in the sky and fire in her chest.

CHAPTER EIGHT

SURVIVE

Coming to the city of Vale was the best decision Roman had ever made. The place was full of rubes. If he had grown up on these streets, he never would have had to fall in with a crime lord like Lil' Miss Malachite in the first place. Anyone with natural talent, a devious mind, lofty ambition, and bankrupt morals could take, take, take whatever they wanted.

In other words: him. Roman could feel it. He was home.

The only thing standing in his way was the fact that the police had a much lower tolerance for criminals than Mistral did. Apparently it had some kind of reputation to uphold as a light to other Kingdoms throughout Remnant, blah blah blah. To be honest, Roman had stopped paying attention to his real estate agent as she bragged about the low crime rates, good schools, and thriving art and music scene downtown. He just wanted to be in the middle of the action.

"It's impressive, isn't it?" His agent, Ms. Burgundy, joined him at the window of the penthouse suite she was showing him. "This is the best view of Beacon Academy anywhere in the city."

Roman squinted at it. "Architecture seems a bit outdated."

"We call it classic, in my line of work. I always thought it seemed magical, like something out of a storybook." She sighed. "I always dreamed of going to Beacon Academy."

"You wanted to be a Huntress?"

"Doesn't every kid want to grow up to be a Huntsman or Huntress?"

Only in my nightmares, he thought.

"I'm guessing that didn't work out," he said.

Her face fell. "No. I washed out of combat school."

"It isn't for everyone. You have to play to your strengths. And if you're lucky, you realize exactly what you want, what you're destined for—and you grab it." He made a fist and clenched it.

"I guess real estate was my true calling." She laughed.

"I guess so. I'll take it."

Her face lit up. "You will? Don't you want to know how much it costs?"

"Doesn't matter. Because I know what I want." He winked at her. She giggled.

In fact, he knew exactly how much it cost, and it was going to wipe out his illicit savings—even though of course he'd avoided paying for his passage from Mistral and food along the way. But Roman believed in going big, and he needed that incentive to get out there and get to work. Nothing motivated you more than hunger.

Going to work meant learning the ins and outs of every neighborhood—essentially casing it out for criminal opportunities. He knew a little bit about the players in Vale, thanks to Lil' Miss, but he needed to see how they controlled their territory.

Figure out how to exploit their weaknesses. Then take over their operations.

So Roman played the tourist. He walked around the city. Visited businesses. Picked out the crooks. Asked subtle questions. He watched. He studied. He planned.

And when he was ready, he made his first move. He could have started small by robbing a grocery store or stealing a car, but that's what any penny-ante crook would do. That wasn't Roman, not anymore—not here. So his plan was to hold up the First Bank of Vale.

A little fish in a big ocean could still make a big splash. Particularly when the ruling crime syndicates thrived by staying under the radar.

He set out for the bank early on his seventh day in Vale with a spring in his step. He had empty pockets and an empty stomach, but not for long.

On a busy weekday morning just before lunch hour, the sidewalks were crammed with people going about their business— which made it easier for Roman to go about *his* business.

As he passed a kid walking while reading his Scroll, Roman stuck his cane out to trip him. Then he whirled and caught the hapless pedestrian before he ate pavement.

"Whoa. Thanks! That was clumsy of me," the boy said.

"My pleasure." Roman tipped his hat. "Have a nice day."

"You too!"

On the next block, without breaking stride, Roman plucked out the cash from the wallet he'd lifted from his mark and tossed the wallet in a trash bin. At some point, when the kid reached for the wallet in his coat pocket, he'd come up with Roman's calling card, imprinted with the words I WAS ROBBED BY ROMAN TORCHWICK.

Roman used the money to buy breakfast—not every transaction had to be illegal—and picked up a little extra money picking some more pockets. It might have seemed greedy to steal from innocent people when he was planning to make a big withdrawal from the bank, but it made a good warm-up, and taking advantage of people always put a smile on his face.

There it was. The First Bank of Vale, another example of "classic" architecture. The tall columns lining the front entrance and large stained-glass windows gave the two-story building a grandiose appearance. That was one of the biggest differences between Vale and Mistral. In Vale, they chose form over function, perhaps because they had the luxury of more territory to spread out over.

That was it: luxury. Everything in the city was planned and intentional, from the clean sidewalks and paved streets to the buildings reaching for the sky. Whereas in Mistral, you built wherever you could, and cities were defined more by accident than intent. Alleys were more trafficked than roads, at least by those who worked best under the cover of darkness.

In that sense, Vale and Mistral were like mirrors of each other, one a place of openness and light, the other a place of secrecy and shadows.

Of course Roman knew that in both cases, it was all just a facade, just as it was with people. Every place, and every person, existed in an equilibrium between light and dark, good and evil.

He had been walking that line his whole life, and that was why he would succeed here as much as he had back in Mistral. More so, because he wouldn't have anyone holding him back.

Roman opened the front door of the bank and held it for an elderly woman just leaving.

"Oh, thank you, young man. Such a gentleman."

Roman grinned. "My pleasure. Have a nice day."

"You too."

Oh, I will, Roman thought as he entered the building. He had been here before already, to take pictures with his Scroll, which he had scrutinized for several days, along with the blueprints he had copied at the city planning office.

He got into the short line of customers and sized up the situation. It was just after noon, so only two of the six teller windows were open, the others out on their lunch break. There were only two security guards, positioned at the bank entrance and beside the vault in a cage behind the teller windows. Roman counted four cameras: one fixed on the teller windows, one fixed on the vault, and two scanning the entire room angled to capture both the entrance and the customer service area. Another bank employee was seated at a desk on the side. And all told, there were about a dozen customers, half of them in line with Roman.

He took a deep breath. *You got this, Roman.*

When it was his turn at the head of the line, he was directed to window six. He was a bit surprised to be greeted by a Faunus man with pointed black dog ears jutting from his lanky black hair.

"Good afternoon. Thank you for choosing First Bank. How can I help you today?" the man asked.

Roman put his cane on the counter and rested both hands atop it.

"I would like all of your money, please."

The man stared at him. "Ha, good one," he said, a mildly puzzled look on his face.

Roman looked back at him and didn't say a word.

"Wait. Seriously?" His eyes flicked to one of the security guards. "Are you robbing the bank?"

"That's the general idea. So come on, make it snappy."

"Shouldn't you have, like, a mask or something? To hide your identity?"

"You watch a lot of movies."

"I do, yeah."

"Well, thanks for your concern, but I'm good. I know what I'm doing."

"There hasn't been a bank robbery in the city in, like, forever. Hey, do you have a gun?"

Roman looked around. "Is he kidding me with this?" He read the name on the teller's name badge. "Fred, let me guess: You're new here."

Fred bobbed his head. "I am! This is my first job. I just graduated in the spring."

"Congratulations," Roman said dryly. "Look, just hand over the money."

The kid looked at him expectantly.

Roman rolled his eyes. "And nobody gets hurt."

Fred smiled. Then the smile faded and he leaned closer to the counter and whispered conspiratorially. "I'm not supposed to."

"Of course you're not supposed to!" People looked at him when he raised his voice. He calmed himself down. "That's why this is a robbery."

Fred leaned back. "Ohhhhhhh. Right."

"Could you move a little faster? Kind of in a hurry here." Roman glanced back at the guard. The guard was watching him now. Great.

Roman picked up his cane and flipped the gun side up.

The teller looked at it curiously.

"Is that . . ." His eyes widened. "He has a gun!" He ducked under the counter.

Roman sighed. Then he turned and pointed his cane up. "Good afternoon! This is a holdup. Everyone drop to the floor and don't move."

About half of the customers looked up in panic, while the others ignored him. The security guard by the door pulled an earbud out of his ear and headed for Roman, fumbling for his gun.

"Hellooooo? This is not a drill." Roman fired. With a bang, fireworks shot out of the tip of his cane and a moment later, pieces of the ceiling drifted downward.

That got everyone's attention. Several people screamed and rushed toward the door. No one dropped to the floor like he had demanded.

"Why doesn't anyone ever listen?" In Mistral, people knew how to be robbed. It must have been a more common occurrence there than it was in Vale. Mistral banks didn't even care about it anymore, since insurance covered everything, and sometimes they were even complicit with the crooks—their way of getting out of paying protection money. That's why the gangsters in Mistral called robberies "economic stimulus." Who cared whether the people spending the money were citizens or crooks? It was all good for business, as long as the money stayed in Mistral.

The guard broke into a run and drew his gun. He planted himself and crouched, exactly the way an action hero would in a movie. He trained his gun on Roman. "Drop the weapon!"

Roman lowered his cane and leveled it at the guard. It was a good old-fashioned showdown. From the corner of his eye, Roman noted the other guard leaving his post at the vault to try to sneak up on him. All four security cameras were now trained on the unfolding action.

"Don't make me shoot," the guard said.

"Do your worst," Roman replied.

The guard squeezed the trigger. Roman lunged with his cane and tapped the side of the gun to push it slightly to the left, as he also moved a step to the right. The shot missed Roman and glass broke somewhere behind him.

Roman flicked his cane up, knocking the gun out of the guard's hand. It flew, hit the marble floors, and skittered away.

"That really was your worst," Roman said. "Unless that was your best."

He swiveled his cane around, hooking the man's wrist with the curved handle. He pulled the guard toward him and kicked his stomach at the same time. Bone snapped as the guard's wrist and a rib broke. The man spun away from the impact, screaming in agony before landing in a heap. He curled up on himself and continued wailing.

"Shut up!" Roman aimed his gun—

"Freeze!"

Roman turned toward the second guard.

"Teaching moment. If you'd shot me instead of yelling—" Roman broke off and fired, hitting the guard's hand. He dropped the gun with a yelp.

These guys were lightweights. It was a wonder the city hadn't been taken over by crime lords by now.

Roman was already starting to like it here.

The guard raised his hands in the air, the universal sign of "I'm in way over my head."

"Now." Roman hopped onto the counter and leaned over it, pressing the tip of his cane to Fred's head. The boy looked like he was finally ready to take the whole situation seriously. "My. Money."

Roman turned slowly, pointing his gun at all the customers, who were finally lying on the floor facedown with their hands on the backs of their heads. Everyone seemed to have seen the same movies about bank robberies. What a time saver.

"In fact, that goes for everyone. I'm going to collect all your money. Wallets. Jewelry. Scrolls. Spare change. Come on, empty your pockets. If you have chewing gum, I want that, too."

Roman spoke to the second guard. "I want all the cash in the vault, too. Take those three with you." Roman gestured to two women and a young boy.

The guard and the others climbed to their feet uncertainly.

Roman cocked the gun again. They hurried off.

Roman heard sirens in the distance. Vale's finest in blue were on their way.

Roman pointed to another bank employee. "You. Lock the doors."

"At least let the people out," the man said.

"Relax, you'll all be fine, as long as I get my money." He looked at the clock above the door. "The service here is terrible."

Before the banker could lock the door, it opened and two people walked in: a man with long silver hair and a woman with no hair at all. They were dressed for a fight. The man's sleeveless shirt was made of bands of silver; matching silver bands around his wrists were bright against his dark skin. He had a belt loaded with small pouches and his loose-fitting pants had many pockets. Combat boots with steel toes completed the ensemble.

His bald companion was outfitted in a black tank top and short red jacket, crisscrossed with bandoliers loaded with dust vials. She had a pleated leather skirt over black leggings and mud-spattered, red high-tops. Iridescent lines spiraled down each of her cotton-white arms.

Huntsmen.

The pair took a moment to assess the situation—they clearly had walked in unaware that there was a robbery in progress.

"We're closed," Roman said. "Come back later."

"What's going on here?" the man said. The woman assumed a fighting stance, holding what looked like a kid's slingshot.

"You're cute, but you're slow, Roch," she said.

He retrieved a metal rod from his belt. One end of the weapon had rows of wicked spikes on it, and the other end had three flexible claws. He pressed a button and the rod extended to his height. The claws opened and closed.

Roman hopped down from the counter. "I don't have time for this," he said.

"Neither do we. The sooner we stop you, the sooner we can deposit our checks." She zipped toward Roman. He fired at her three times as she zigzagged, only just missing her each time. Before he could correct for her speed and direction, she was leaping into the air and coming at him with a corkscrew kick. He sidestepped her, and as she landed, he hooked her right ankle with his cane.

He started to pull, but she lifted her leg and spun around on her left foot—pulling him instead. Roman went flying, but he twisted himself around and came down facing her, sliding backward a few steps.

Almost too late, he saw the other Huntsman charging toward him like a bull. Roman jumped aside. As Roch went by, he held up his weapon. It extended even longer and the claw on its end grabbed Roman's right wrist in it like a vise. Roch stopped and braced himself, holding on to it and keeping Roman from lifting his cane.

Roman aimed his cane at the man and fired. The sudden flash of fireworks made the man drop his weapon and stagger backward, covering his eyes. The claw on the end loosened and Roman shook it off.

He turned and saw the Huntress aiming at him with her slingshot, a vial loaded.

"Nice toy," Roman said.

She let loose and the vial flew toward Roman. He shot it easily and it shattered in front of him. Tiny crystals exploded from it and settled over his hands and coat.

He looked down at the red and green powder covering his hands. He tried to shake it off him, but it only stuck.

Then it started popping. He felt pinpricks of pain wherever the Dust crystals burst and dissipated. Another vial crashed and broke at his feet, and he found he couldn't step back because his shoes were stuck fast to the floor.

Roman shot straight down and the flooring crumbled, releasing his shoes. He backed up slowly, as the two Huntsmen closed in on them.

"Sweet work, Kandi," Roch said.

"Not bad yourself. It's kind of refreshing to fight a bad guy instead of a Grimm for a change."

Roman scanned the room. The civilians had moved to the other side of the room, clustered together watching the battle, some of them streaming it from their Scrolls. Cop cars were parked outside, officers standing around waiting for the Huntsmen to do their job for them. It was time for him to end this.

"You're pretty good. Where'd you learn to fight?" Kandi asked.

"Mistral," Roman said.

"Which combat school?"

"Self-study." Roman narrowed his eyes, then he went for Roch, swinging his cane at him.

Roch blocked the swing with his metal staff, and swung the spiked end at Roman. The guy was strong, but consequently his style was somewhat clumsy. He counted on his strength to get the job done.

Roman knew how to use that against him.

Roman was faster and more nimble. He continued to parry and thrust, while slowly moving to put Roch between Roman and Kandi. So that when she fired another Dust vial at him, he was perfectly positioned. He aimed and fired at the vial—but he didn't shoot a projectile, only a burst of compressed air from the tip of his cane, which redirected the vial at Roch. Just as he was swinging his staff.

His weapon made contact with the Dust vial, which broke and splattered a green, goo-like substance over him. He looked back at Kandi with both surprise and disappointment as the substance hardened into jagged crystals all over his body, immobilizing him.

As Kandi tended to her partner, Roman deployed the grappling hook on his cane. It latched onto the crossed bandolier; he began reeling her in like a fish.

Kandi reached behind her and tried to free herself as she was pulled toward Roman. Just before she reached him, she unfastened the bandolier and rolled free. Roman fell backward from the sudden shift in weight, but he had her Dust vials.

She faced him and held up her slingshot before her.

"What are you going to do with that?" Roman dangled the bandolier over his head. "I have your ammo."

She squinted at him, and the belt in his hand began vibrating.

No, it was the glass vials that were vibrating. One of them, which held a yellow powder, cracked.

Roman studied Kandi. Her weapon wasn't just a slingshot, he realized. It was made of some kind of metal; the shape of it reminded him of a tuning fork. And it was vibrating.

She was somehow using it to generate a high-frequency sound wave. A windowpane cracked. The yellow vial burst and when the Dust touched Roman's hand, he felt first a spark, like a bad electric shock, and then arcs of lightning began to crackle across the grains.

Roman dropped the belt and kicked it away as more vials began popping. A red one burst, spraying small fireballs into the air. A blue one flash-froze the surface of the floor around it.

"This is weird," Roman said.

He heard a high-pitched whine now, and the stained-glass window behind him shattered, sending a rainbow of deadly glass shards into the air.

And the Dust crystals holding Roch fast began to crack and crumble.

"Time to go," Roman said.

He spun around and swooped up the bags of Lien. "Thanks," he said to Fred. He used his grappling hook to propel himself up to the broken window at the back of the bank. No cop cars down on the street—yet.

He turned and doffed his hat to Kandi and Roch as police officers finally swarmed in and surrounded the two Huntsmen.

"My heroes," he said. He jumped backward out of the window and to freedom.

Back in his apartment, Roman watched the Vale News Network

on his brand-new seventy-inch TV while he ate the most delicious meal of takeout barbecue ribs he'd ever had.

The news anchor, Lisa Lavender, was calling the afternoon's robbery of the First Bank of Vale "one of the most brazen displays of lawlessness" she'd ever witnessed in all her years of reporting.

"Stop, you're making me blush." He made a note to send Lisa some flowers, signed to his "biggest fan."

"One of the biggest questions stumping police is: Who was that unmasked man? Though he made no attempt to hide his identity—even seeming to welcome the attention—he has no criminal record, in Vale or anywhere else in Remnant.

"However, we believe we have the name of Vale's newest criminal."

The video cut to Lisa interviewing one of the people who Roman had pickpocketed early that day.

"You reported earlier today that your wallet was missing, isn't that right, Mr. Zhu?"

"I'm going to be on TV?" Zhu asked.

"We'll see," Lisa said. "You were pickpocketed and you found something . . . ?"

"Oh, that's right. Instead of my wallet, I found this in my pocket." He held up a black card with white lettering on it. The camera focused in on it while Lisa read it aloud.

"You've been robbed by Roman Torchwick."

Video cut back to the studio.

"In fact, this 'Roman Torchwick' pickpocketed dozens of people in a path to the bank, leaving his calling card in place of their precious cash. Police are hoping to track his path to the bank from reports—"

"You don't think I thought of that?" Roman shouted at the TV. "I thought of everything!"

"If it does, indeed, turn out that he is also responsible for the bank robbery, that raises some baffling questions as to his motive. Perhaps this Torchwick was more interested in people knowing his identity than he was in the money itself."

Roman raised a glass to her. "Two birds with one stone, dear."

"Meanwhile, the Huntsmen who were apprehended and initially charged with the robbery, Roch Szalt and Kandi Floss, are still being fined for destruction of public property and reckless endangerment. This isn't the first time they've been reprimanded for using excessive force and gross misconduct. The Vale Huntsmen Guild reportedly is considering suspending their licenses."

"Three birds!" Roman said.

"We spoke to a local expert on Huntsmen, Professor Ozpin, headmaster of Beacon Academy, about his take on their actions today."

The TV showed a man with gray hair and dark spectacles seated in front of a large window looking out over the city of Vale. Roman looked out his own window toward the school's campus on the edge of Beacon Cliff.

"We hold Huntsmen to a higher standard because they wield more power than most citizens, power which can be just as dangerous as it can be a force for good, if used maliciously or carelessly. I do believe Mr. Szalt and Ms. Floss operated with the best of intentions, and I hope they can learn from this experience and come out of it stronger. Accepting a license means accepting the sacred responsibility of protecting others—from anything that threatens their safety, whether by humans or Grimm."

He turned to face the camera. "One more thing. Roman Torchwick—"

Roman almost choked on his drink.

"I assume that you are new to Vale. You got away today, but be assured, we will be watching you. And the next time you cross a Huntsman, things may not go as easily for you."

The program cut back to Lavender. "Inspiring words from Professor Ozpin. Professor Lionheart, headmaster of Szalt and Floss's former school, Haven Academy in Mistral, could not be reached for comment in time for this story. More on this developing story as we have it."

The program cut to a shot of a stately mansion with a fire truck in front of it. "We now return live to the Vanille Estate, home of Vale city manager Jimmy—" Roman switched off the TV.

Well, things hadn't gone quite as planned, but they had turned out even better than he expected. You couldn't complain if you had a roof over your head and a full belly at the end of the day, and he had accomplished what he had set out to do: announce his presence in Vale, establish his intentions, and send a message to both local law enforcement and the crime syndicates. There was a new crook in town.

Roman looked around his empty apartment, and for the briefest of moments he missed his old crew. He missed Chameleon. Moments like this were meant to be shared, and Brick, Mortar, and

Rusty would have been toasting him right now for making those Huntsmen look like fools and pulling off a massive crime in broad daylight, under the noses of the police.

Roman put down his empty glass and raised the bottle instead.

"Cheers to me," he said.

Tomorrow, he would pick another bank and do it all over again.

CHAPTER NINE

ARRIVAL

"Welcome to your new home," Mama said.

Trivia and her mother walked up a winding flagstone path toward a wide building that resembled a small, cozy castle. The most prominent features in its pink-granite facade were three tall, arched windows, reflecting the morning sun. A short, square tower with pinnacled corners rose above the center window; at its base was an arched entryway with LADY BROWNING'S PREPARATORY ACADEMY FOR GIRLS carved into it.

This will never be my home. Trivia wrinkled her nose. She turned around, calling Mama's bluff. They just wanted to scare her into behaving better, being the daughter they wanted.

But Mama grabbed hold of Trivia's sleeve and pulled her gently toward the entrance. Trivia shook her head frantically. *I'm sorry! I'm sorry!*

Her mother looked away.

Trivia snatched her arm back from her. *I'm not sorry.* You set a little fire in your house, and the next thing you know, your parents were sending you away. Well, maybe things wouldn't be so bad here. This is what she had wanted, right? To be out and on her own? There were other girls here. Trivia would make friends.

A girl Trivia's age met them at the entrance, holding open one of the red double doors. Her ghost-white face contrasted dramatically with the dark blue of her jacket. Trivia surveyed the rest of the uniform: white blouse, gold scarf and matching knee-length dress, black tights and high-heeled boots. The only jewelry she wore was a silver pin over her heart adorned with a triple spiral.

Trivia held up a hand and waved awkwardly. The other girl's flat expression didn't change, but her eyes dipped to take in Trivia and her princess pajamas, her only clothes that hadn't burned in the fire. Mama had said there was no point in buying her a new outfit because the school would provide everything she needed.

The girl's right eyebrow twitched, but she betrayed no emotion. She turned smartly on her heel and led them down a corridor lined with group photos of girls all wearing the same uniform, and the same expressionless faces. *Former classes?* Trivia figured. *Looks like they know how to have a good time here.*

The girl stopped in front of an elegant door, knocked once, and departed. As she passed, she murmured something under her breath so only Trivia could hear. It was so low, she wasn't even certain she had heard anything, and it wasn't until the door opened a moment later that Trivia realized the girl had said, "Good luck."

Another uniformed girl, this one with tan skin and close-cropped black hair, opened the door. Trivia and her mother stepped into a combination office and parlor outfitted with extravagant furniture: knickknack tables, credenzas, a velvet reclining couch, a vintage love seat. Portraits and tapestries hung around the room, and an entire wall was decorated with framed photos of glamorous women with personal notes and autographs.

This office did remind Trivia of home, but not one of the

rooms they used to welcome visitors. Some furniture was meant to be admired but never touched. Trivia noticed Mama appraising each piece, a twinkle of envy in her eyes.

From across the room, an older woman rose from her broad desk like a living monolith, every bit as imposing as the school itself. She was extraordinarily tall. Granted, everyone was taller than Trivia, but this woman was easily six feet, and thin. She reminded Trivia of runway models in the Vale fashion shows she used to watch.

The headmistress, too, wore the same jacket, blouse, and dress as the students Trivia had seen, but on her, the outfit was stunning. Smart, sexy, and a little dangerous. *This* was how it was meant to be worn. In comparison, the girls looked like they were dressing up in their mother's wardrobe.

The woman glided across the room and clasped her hands together warmly. She was even more impressive up close. Her gray-blond hair was swept up in a beehive, only adding to her height. Her fair skin was dusted with gold powder that sparkled when she moved, and dark eyeliner exaggerated her wide, piercing lavender eyes. Bright red lipstick dared you to look away.

She made Trivia abruptly conscious of her unwashed, unkempt appearance and her ratty, soot-smudged pajamas.

"Welcome back, Carmel. It's so good to see you, and to see you doing so well," the woman said.

"The school hasn't changed," Mama said. "Neither have you."

"I'm glad you haven't forgotten your training."

Trivia stared at her mother. She had attended this school? Trivia recalled that her mother had a gold spiral pin like the one on the students' uniforms, but she only wore it on special occasions.

"You must be Trivia," the tall woman said.

If I must, I must, Trivia thought.

Mama jostled Trivia with her elbow. Trivia shot her an annoyed look and then she curtsied, as sarcastically as she could manage.

"Oh my, that won't do," the woman said. "You have certainly come to the right place. And just at the right time, from the look of things."

"Trivia, this is Lady Beatrix Browning."

"My girls call me Lady Beat," the woman said.

"Jimmy and I are so grateful that you could fit her into the school halfway through the year," Mama said.

"Your generous donations over the years have benefited the girls so much," Lady Beat said. She turned her attention back to Trivia. "Your mother tells me that you don't like to talk."

Trivia scrunched up her face. She shook her head, touched her mouth, and shrugged.

"Will that be a problem?" Mama asked.

"Oh no. In fact, quite the opposite. As you know, one of our core principles is that it is better to be seen, not heard." She winked at Trivia. "And often it's better not to be seen at all."

Trivia found herself smiling despite herself. Lady Beat was charming, she'd give her that.

"Well . . . good," Mama said uncertainly. "What happens next?"

"Now you go and Trivia stays. She will be measured for her school uniform and while the girls prepare it for her, I will administer a short aptitude test to figure out what she's good at, and where she fits in. Some girls are natural leaders, but others are better suited to following." She considered Trivia. "They both have their place and their value."

Lady Beat gestured to the girl by the door. "Please show Mrs. Vanille out."

Mama studied Trivia for a moment, various emotions flitting across her face until she settled on tenderness. She wrapped her arms around Trivia. Trivia did not return the hug.

"I'll call and write," Mama said. "Try to be good here. I . . ."

Trivia waited, blinking back tears.

"I'll miss you."

Her mother brushed away imaginary tears and headed for the door.

Trivia drew in a deep breath.

"Welcome home, Ms. Vanille," Lady Beat said.

When she said it, Trivia almost started to believe it.

CHAPTER TEN

RIVAL

Roman stepped out of his apartment building holding a white paper bag and his cane. He spotted the unmarked police car parked across the street and sauntered toward it. The cops inside watched as he approached the car, opened the back door, and slid in. He slammed the door shut and noted there were no handles on the inside.

"Good morning, gents," Roman said.

"Uh," said the driver.

"You're Roman Torchwick?" said the other. "The guy who robbed the bank yesterday?"

"That's right. You got me, boys."

"Great." The driver scratched his head. "So, I'm Dunn and this is Looney. We have some questions?"

"Yeah. Starting with: What's in that bag?" Looney said.

"Almost forgot. This is for you." Roman handed a bag forward. Looney flinched, but Dunn grabbed the bag.

"You're turning yourself in *and* you brought us a present?" Dunn opened the bag before Looney could stop him.

"What's wrong with you, Dan?" Looney said. "That could have exploded or something."

"With me in the car?" Roman tsked and shook his head. "Just a peace offering."

"Donuts!" Dunn said excitedly.

"Don't—"

Dunn bit into a donut and started chewing. Red jelly dribbled down his chin.

"Eat that," Looney finished. "He probably poisoned them."

"You're a very suspicious man. You should be a detective," Roman said.

"Don't get him started," Dunn said, his mouth full.

Looney took out a powdered donut and sniffed it. He gently squeezed it and then rubbed some of the powdered sugar between his fingers and thumb. "These are fresh."

"Nothing gets past you," Roman said.

Looney looked at the bag, which was marked with the logo Dough to Go. He peered out the windshield at the DOUGH TO GO shop just across the street.

"I picked them up just this morning," Roman said.

"How'd you do that? We've been staking out your place since last night," Looney said.

"It was disappointingly easy," Roman said.

He had noticed the car from his window before he went to bed, and it was still there in the morning when he woke up. But he certainly wasn't going to confront the boys in blue before he had his morning cup of coffee.

And he'd thought it would be nice to remind them that he was always one step ahead of them. Of course other than the beautiful view in his apartment, Roman had chosen his building because it offered many different exits, some less obvious than others. For some reason the many people who could afford to live there were also the kind of people who wanted to come and go unnoticed.

Looney scowled. "Then why turn yourself in?"

"I've realized the error of my ways and want to give up my life of crime, et cetera et cetera." Roman laughed. "Kidding, of course. I just figured we would cut to the chase. Actually, skip the chase entirely."

"And you aren't going to resist?" Dunn said. "Matte, don't eat all those. You didn't even want them." He grabbed the donut bag from his partner. "Aw, you ate my favorite kind."

"Look, we have the same goal here. You want to get the praise for bringing me in. And I want to talk to your *boss*." Roman winked.

"All right. If you say so . . ." Dunn started the car.

The car drove several blocks over to the police station—then past it, picking up speed. Roman smiled to himself. Just as he'd thought. These guys either weren't real cops or they were accepting pay from someone else. Whatever their job, they were terrible at it. Roman would never want someone like them working for him. This was why he didn't want *anyone* working for him—good help was hard to find.

They kept driving north, into the commercial district, the beating heart of the city. Roman sat back and pulled out a cigar.

Looney looked at him in the rearview mirror. "No smoking."

Torchwick lit the cigar with a grin. "Arrest me."

"I have asthma," Looney grumbled, and lowered his window.

Roman puffed on his cigar and blew a stream of smoke toward

the front of the vehicle. Both of them coughed. Roman chuckled and enjoyed the ride.

After ten minutes, the car parked behind a cozy restaurant named Just Right.

"End of the line," Dunn said. The two men exited and Looney opened Roman's door for him. "Come with us."

"I didn't know this was a date. I should have brought flowers instead of donuts." Roman checked the time on his pocket watch. "Little early for dinner, though. I haven't got an appetite yet."

"Get in there." Looney shoved Roman toward the door. Roman shot him a dirty look. "Sorry," Dunn said.

"'Sorry'? Stop treating him like a guest. He's a prisoner, remember? And if the boss doesn't want him, we'll turn him in for the reward," Looney said.

"Reward, huh? How much is it? Maybe I'll turn myself in. Again," Roman said.

Roman stepped through the back entrance of the restaurant and found himself in a kitchen. It was nearly empty except for a man wearing an apron and chef hat, holding a butcher knife. He was taller than Roman, wiry, and strong looking.

"Carnation, take his weapon," Looney said.

Roman held up his cane. "This thing? It's just for walking."

"We saw the video of the robbery."

Roman hesitated, but then he handed Melodic Cudgel over. Carnation put it in a drawer below the counter and locked it. Then he jerked his head toward the double doors leading into the dining room. He slowly sharpened his blade and followed Roman with his eyes as he walked by.

The dining room was mostly dark, since it wasn't open for business this early in the morning. The gaudy decor with fancy crystal chandeliers, gold trim, and mirrors everywhere suggested this was a place that you needed reservations for, probably at least a year in advance. The tables had white tablecloths and elaborate glass centerpieces, already set with silverware. It was clear where Roman was meant to go: One table was lit in the center of the room, with a heavyset man in an expensive suit waiting at a table for two.

The cops nudged Roman over.

"Roman Torchwick." The man's voice rumbled. He had shoulder-length black hair streaked with gray and a scruffy beard that almost hid his double chin and ruddy complexion. He had triangular eyes, the color of stormy clouds. But most notably, the top of his left ear was missing. It had healed in a ragged line, suggesting that it had been bitten off, rather than sliced or shot.

Roman bowed. "And you must be Hei Xiong."

Xiong looked disapprovingly at the two cops.

"We didn't tell him anything, sir," Dunn said.

"You're new here, but you already know my name?"

Roman sat down across from him and kicked his feet up on the table.

"Of course I recognize you. You're the head of the Xiong crime family. I was hoping to meet you. I figured my stunt yesterday would get the attention of the biggest crime boss in Vale."

"That it did." Xiong slapped Roman's feet off the table. The gesture was careless, but he packed a lot of strength in that meaty hand of his. Roman lurched up and sat straight in his seat.

"Show some respect," Looney said.

Xiong held up a hand. "I've dealt with people like you before, Torchwick. You like to put on a big act, pretend like you know everything, have it all worked out. But you're just making it up as you go along, going through life scared someone will figure it out."

Roman forced himself to keep smiling. "That's fascinating. Do you charge by the hour for this service? Because if we're going to keep talking like this I'll need to rob another bank."

Xiong laughed once, a loud barking sound that grated on Roman's ears. "We have a funny guy here. Some kind of clown."

He held up a hand and gestured toward the kitchen. Roman avoided turning around as the doors opened and solid footsteps approached, but he was ready for anything. His hands tightened into fists.

The chef stepped up to the table and dropped two heavy bowls in front of them. Roman looked distastefully at the gray slop in his bowl.

"Oatmeal. The best way to start the day. I've had oatmeal for breakfast for over thirty years." Xiong picked up a heaping spoonful of it and shoveled it into his mouth. A glob of it rolled down his beard. Roman tried to stir the muck in his bowl, but it was like trying to mix setting cement.

The chef eyed him and shifted his grip on the butcher knife in his right hand.

Roman tasted a small spoonful of the oatmeal. It tasted like mud. He swallowed it and smiled. "Delicious. Hearty."

"I brought you here to ask your intentions in Vale. What are you doing on my turf?"

"It isn't just your turf anymore." Roman sniffed. "I'm taking over."

"How? Robbing banks? You'll never get away with another job like that. You got lucky, Torchwick. They didn't see you coming, and then those buffoons got in the way and made an even bigger mess than you did.

"You can't just waltz in here and start breaking the law. There's a protocol. We do things a certain way. I don't know what it's like wherever you come from— Where'd you come from, anyway?"

"Mistral," Roman said.

Xiong tossed down his spoon. "That explains it! I think you'll find that we're a little more refined here. We aren't just crime bosses—we're businessmen. I already have an arrangement with the banks. You rob them, and you rob me."

Xiong took another bite of food and chewed it slowly. He swallowed and pointed his drippy spoon at Roman, jabbing it toward him to punctuate each word: "No. One. Robs. Me."

Roman put down his spoon. "I consider myself a businessman, too."

Xiong shook his head. "You aren't getting it. Your business is my business now. If you want to stay in Vale, you work for me."

Roman considered the crime boss across from him. He wasn't too impressed. He'd expected someone on the level of Lil' Miss Malachite, but Xiong wasn't anywhere in the same league with her. He was just a guy who relied on his reputation to do all the work for him.

Roman leaned back in his seat. "Here's my counteroffer. How about *you* work for *me* from now on?"

Xiong laughed again. "You got some spine, Torchwick. I'll give you that. So that's how it's gotta be between us?"

"'Fraid so."

"You *should* be afraid. Fear is a powerful survival mechanism. It lets us know when we're in danger, in a situation we aren't equipped to handle. Without fear, you sometimes have to learn your lessons the hard way."

Xiong turned his spoon slowly. In the shiny silver surface, Roman saw Dunn and Looney reaching for him. Roman slipped under the table before they could grab him, then stood up, lifting it onto his back and flipping it toward them. They dove to either side out of the way.

The next thing Roman knew, Xiong had grabbed him in a tight bear hug. He squirmed, but he couldn't break free. The intense pressure on his chest made it harder for him to breathe.

"Take him," Xiong said. The cops advanced toward him. Then Looney opened his mouth.

"Mr. Xiong, I don't feel so—" His eyes rolled up in his head and he collapsed.

"What happened to him?" Xiong asked.

"The donuts," Dunn said. "You *did* poison them."

"Of course I did," Roman said.

Dunn collapsed onto his partner.

"Are they dead?" Xiong asked.

"Just sleeping for a few hours. They'll wake up with a headache. Unless I mixed up the powders again. I really should label them."

"Carnation, you're up." Xiong shoved Roman away. He staggered and caught himself on one knee, trying to catch his breath. His arms and chest ached.

The chef slashed at him with his big knife. Roman dove and

rolled out of the way. As he came up, he swept his leg out and the chef went down, still holding on to his knife.

Roman popped back up and walked around the chef. The man brandished his blade. He lunged at Roman several times. Roman jumped back as the knife cut across his chest. His Aura protected him from a deadly cut, but his shirt and jacket didn't fare so well.

"I'll send you the dry cleaning bill." Roman peeled off his shredded jacket. "Better yet, I'll rob the dry cleaners."

Roman twisted up his jacket and swung it toward Carnation. The chef swiped at him, and Roman managed to get the blade caught in his jacket. He tore it away from the man. It flew across the room and disappeared behind a table.

Roman threw his jacket aside. "That's better. Now we'll settle this with our fists."

He rolled up his left sleeve, then his right. He began hopping around Carnation and was just about to throw a right hook when Xiong shouted, "Stop!"

Roman froze. He and Carnation exchanged a confused glance and turned to look at Xiong.

"Why didn't you just tell me you were sent here by Lil' Miss Malachite?" Xiong said.

Roman raised an eyebrow. "Pardon?"

"She's reneging on the deal, is that it? Trying to horn in on my territory? We had an agreement. We operate only in our own Kingdoms. There's plenty to go around that way. And now this—" He gestured at Roman. "One of her little spiders crawls into my house."

"I don't work for Lil' Miss," Roman said, his voice hard.

Xiong grabbed his right wrist and held on tight. Roman pulled but he couldn't break free of his viselike grip.

"This says otherwise." Xiong pointed out the small spider tattoo on Roman's forearm.

"I used to work for Lil' Miss," Roman said. "But I decided it was time to start my own criminal empire."

"That's nonsense. Isn't that nonsense, Carnation?"

"Spiders are for life, sir," Carnation said.

"Meaning you're lying and you work for her, or"—Xiong lifted Roman up by his wrist—"you ran away. In which case, Lil' Miss is probably looking for you."

"There's a third option," Roman said.

"What's that?"

"You're a moron." Roman grabbed on to Xiong's arm with his free hand and pulled himself up to kick the man in the face. Xiong bellowed, but he didn't drop Roman.

"You little punk!" He held Roman up to his eye level. Roman's wrist was starting to hurt and he couldn't feel his hand anymore. But he was happy to see his heel had left a red imprint on Xiong's thick forehead.

"When you see Malachite, give her a message. I know she's been running operations here in Vale, expanding her web throughout Remnant. A museum here, a shipping company there, that's fine. I can look the other way. But make no mistake: This city is mine. I ran out the other syndicates, and I'm the only game in town. Hear me? If she's planning another stunt like your performance yesterday—if she starts interfering in *my* business, there'll be a reckoning.

"We don't need that kind of attention, am I right? And in one day, you've got criminals on the Huntsmen's radar, you've got the cops all riled up. That's not good. And I don't think she wants to go to war with me on top of all the other crime bosses in Mistral. That's just going to make it harder on all of us."

He dropped Roman. Roman managed to catch his balance before falling and shook his right hand to get feeling back in it.

"If she wants to negotiate a new deal and give me a bigger cut, let's talk about it like civilized people, face-to-face." Xiong squished Roman's cheeks with one giant hand and shook his head from side to side. "I hope you enjoyed your visit to Vale. Now get outta here."

Carnation escorted him out of the restaurant, back the way he'd come. On the way he handed Roman his weapon.

"You like working for Xiong?" Roman asked him.

"It's better than *not* working for him," Carnation said. "If you enjoy breathing."

Roman stepped out into the parking lot and the door slammed behind him. He sat on the step, lit a cigar, then massaged his sore wrist. It still showed a red impression of Xiong's hand. Roman rubbed at the spider tattoo.

He didn't work for Lil' Miss anymore, and he would never work for Xiong. But it seemed he needed a new plan if he wanted to carve a place for himself in Vale, something that wouldn't encroach on anyone else's territory.

But first, he needed a new jacket, and he needed to get rid of this tattoo. Fortunately he was in the right part of town.

He made his way back to the strip and looked for the seediest tattoo parlor he could find, where he was pretty sure the spider on his arm wouldn't set off any alarms.

"What can you do with this? Can you remove it?" Roman showed his arm to the tatted-up lady behind the counter.

"Remove your arm?" She reached behind the counter and pulled out a bone saw. "Sure, but it's gonna cost ya. And it's gonna hurt."

Roman frowned. "I was thinking something less drastic. I just want the *tattoo* gone."

"Oh. Right." She looked disappointed and stowed the bone saw away. She studied the spider tattoo for a moment.

"It's good work. Shame to erase work like that." She took out her Scroll and sketched for a few minutes. "Might be easier to rework it. How do you feel about pumpkins?"

She held up her screen to show him a drawing of an evil, grinning face, carved into a pumpkin.

"I like its attitude. You can do that?"

"Pay me enough and I can draw anything you want."

"I'm in," Roman said.

She led him into a dimly lit back room that looked like a surgical theater. A bright spotlight illuminated a chair with a frightening array of straps and buckles.

"It's still gonna hurt, though," she said as she readied her needle.

"It always does when the past catches up to you."

CHAPTER ELEVEN

TRIVIAL PURSUIT

The novelty of living away at Lady Browning's Academy wore off in less than twenty-four hours. Trivia had never thought she'd miss her parents and the bedroom that had been her prison for so long, but it turned out they had at least given her privacy. She hadn't slept a wink in her lumpy single bed in a room with nineteen other teenage girls, snoring and muttering in their sleep. Someone had been crying for an hour, and Trivia had been about to find them and smother them with a pillow when they finally shut up and dozed off.

The same twenty girls had to share a bathroom that seemed to have been designed to cause daily arguments. There was only one large mirror over the sinks, which everyone crowded around in the morning. There were only three stalls. And in the row of six showers, apparently only one provided hot water at any given time, four offered lukewarm water, and one unlucky girl had a cold shower. Today, that girl was Trivia.

Breakfast was bland eggs and dry toast in a bland cafeteria with dozens of bland students. Despite Lady Beat's glorification of girls being seen but not heard, the students at the school were anything but quiet. Trivia had never heard so much *noise* in her entire life.

At first she stood uncertainly with her food tray, looking around the room for a welcoming group or a friendly face who might gesture for her to join them, but no one did. Each time she moved to take an empty seat, she was told, "Oh, we're saving that." The other girls ignored her like she wasn't even there—until she eventually found an empty table and sat by herself. *Then* she became the center of attention, as people snuck looks at her, their expressions an array of amusement, malice, and pity.

Somehow Trivia always ended up alone, even in a crowd.

Granted, she wasn't much of a conversationalist, but she was a great listener. So she listened. She forced down the tasteless food while really feasting on gossip about her schoolmates. She heard about how Roux still slept with her stuffed cat and wet her bed every night and how Celeste had an older boyfriend at Oscuro Combat School. Laurel was the girl who cried herself to sleep every night, and Trivia wasn't the only one who hated her. Veronica was the spoiled daughter of a Vale city councilwoman who had been sent to the school after stealing and trashing her mother's boyfriend's car—there was a lot to unpack there. Erin and Mauve were supposedly a thing again (yay?), the third time they had broken up and gotten back together again this month. They were so romantic and cute together, but would they ever last?

Trivia rolled her eyes.

Of course the other girls also talked about Trivia, some of them loudly enough that she couldn't help but hear them. They all wondered who she was and what she had done. One girl somehow did recognize her as a Vanille, and said she'd heard their mansion had burned down the night before and her parents were dead. Trivia smiled at the thought, setting off another flurry of wild speculation.

Someone said Trivia never spoke, and the girls at her table wondered why that was with increasingly outlandish theories. Another girl claimed that Trivia had lived in her parents' attic, and she was only sent to the school when the police found out—which admittedly had some truth to it. Others criticized every aspect of Trivia's appearance, especially her height and her mismatched eyes.

Trivia made note of everyone who said something meant to hurt her. But when you grew up listening to your parents say cruel things about you, even to your face, comments from strangers lost their sting. She didn't know most of these people yet, and she certainly didn't care about what any of them thought of her, but some of what she overheard might be useful one day.

Mostly, it was interesting for her to study other people. Since the fire, when Neopolitan had disappeared and begun asserting herself more directly, Trivia had become more observant of people's motivations. What people decided to say aloud often said more about them—who they were and what they wanted—than anything else. And most people talk way too much and reveal more than they should.

Keep talking, Trivia thought, chewing her food. *Tell me all your secrets.*

Picking up gossip at mealtimes and in whispered conversations between beds and in the halls was always the highlight of Trivia's day. After three days at the school, she was certain that she was dying—of boredom. She had been understimulated at home, sure, but here not only were students not allowed to leave the grounds without permission, but also they weren't allowed to watch videos or play games, and their reading material was strictly controlled.

She was living her worst nightmare. One morning, Lady Beat was actually instructing them on how to *walk*.

"Remember: posture, girls. Keep your heads high. Backs straight. Chest out," Lady Beat said.

Several girls tittered at that and pushed their bosoms out. Trivia rolled her eyes and focused on keeping her balance.

Slouching had never been much of a problem for Trivia; she was short, so she always tried to stand as tall as possible. But Lady Beat's lessons to teach her girls to be more aware of how they sat and stood and moved, to *listen* to their body and what it was telling them about their feelings (gag), had at least showed Trivia that she did slouch sometimes. When she was depressed or upset, she almost tried to pull herself in, to disappear. And before coming here, she had been depressed and upset a lot.

Of course it was one thing to concentrate on not slouching when you were sitting at your desk, and quite another thing when you were balancing on a tightrope twenty feet in the air, with no net below you. Lady Beat believed in "tough love"—without the love part.

Trivia worked her way across the thin wire with her arms outstretched on either side. Head high. Back straight. Chest out.

She smiled. Okay, that was a little funny.

Surprisingly, thinking about those things helped keep her mind off the fact that she was in danger of falling and prevented her from overthinking every step she took. She strode across the ten-foot gap quickly and seemingly effortlessly, a few feet ahead of the other girls on the other ropes. Trivia gave a deep bow on the other side. Lady Beat led the others in a round of polite clapping. Ladies did not make unnecessary noise, and all the girls were here to learn to be proper ladies.

Which, of course the very notion of that practically made Trivia sick, but she had to admit, she was very, very good at this stuff and she loved it. The physical lessons—learning to study movement to really control yourself and your facial expressions—were some of the few bright spots about living at Lady Browning's Preparatory Academy for Girls. Trivia enjoyed acrobatics classes, ribbon, fencing, even ballet. It was everything else that bored her out of her mind.

The social etiquette. Cooking. Cleaning. Sewing.

Actually, sewing wasn't that bad. But the girls at the school were forced to make clothes they would never wear, high-fashion items that would be sold at boutiques throughout Vale like the ones Trivia used to shoplift from. Meanwhile, they all had to wear the same drab uniforms, since "distraction was a neighbor to destruction," as Lady Beat liked to say.

Trivia missed destruction.

In fact, Trivia actually missed home. A little bit.

The real problem at Lady Browning's Preparatory Academy for Girls was the girls, Trivia thought as the Malachite twins shot angry looks at her for the terrible crime of beating them across the ropes. Melanie and Miltia were the worst of the lot. The popular, pretty girls had singled Trivia out and turned the others against her. So much for having a fresh start and making real friends.

One day, three months after Trivia had arrived, Melanie and Miltia took things too far. Trivia woke up late and discovered she was alone in the dormitory. All the others had snuck out quietly before the alarm went off, and switched off the alarm so she would oversleep. And her uniform was missing, so Trivia had the choice of missing class or showing up late in her pajamas, like a bad dream. But she had a third option: Trivia simply used her Semblance to mask her pajamas and appear in the Lady Beat–approved short dark-blue-colored jacket, white blouse, pleated, calf-length skirt, and boots.

She paid attention when she walked into origami class (really?) to see who was surprised the most, and then she'd followed Melanie and Miltia afterward to where they had stowed her clothes in a maintenance closet. She listened outside the door.

"I don't get it, Miltia. Her clothes are right here where we left them. So where did she get the other outfit?"

"I don't know, Melanie. But I really don't like her already. Do you?"

"As if."

Trivia locked them in. And then, because she didn't know what else to do, she went to Lady Beat.

Big mistake.

Lady Beat kept Trivia waiting outside her office before allowing her inside. Through the glass partitions Trivia could see her working, talking to someone on her Scroll and typing into her computer. She reminded Trivia a lot of her father. Lady Beat finally waved Trivia inside, and she sat across from her desk, an elegant antique like the ones her family collected.

Lady Beat smiled a perfect smile, which would have seemed genuine if Trivia had not known one of the classes at the school was called "The Art of the Smile." This smile conveyed warmth and was meant to encourage feelings of camaraderie, but there was a hint of meanness behind it and a sense that she was merely humoring the child.

Trivia started typing on her Scroll and swiveled the screen around to show it to Lady Beat. The smile cracked slightly.

"Why don't you use the app," Lady Beat said. Not a question.

Trivia managed to suppress a grimace. She pressed her thumb to the screen and the text pulsed. A mechanical female voice read the words aloud: "Melanie and Miltia stole my uniform to make me look bad."

Trivia hated that voice. It made everything she said sound stupid. And it just didn't sound like her. She didn't know how she would sound if she could talk, but it wouldn't be so flat. Trivia had always imagined her voice would be musical, airy and bright, like a flute. Hearing a computer substitute that sounded like those alphabet toys she had played with as a child was worse than keeping quiet.

But Lady Beat had made it clear that if she had something to say, she needed to use the voice app. It wasn't reasonable for her to expect others to read her words for her, or work to comprehend what she was trying to communicate. Her parents had coddled her too long, Lady Beat told her privately, after Carmel Vanille had left, but those days were over now.

Lady Beat did not look surprised to hear Trivia's accusation. Did the girls pull this on new students often?

"And?" She looked Trivia over. "I know about your Semblance, Ms. Vanille. And you know the rules."

Trivia nodded.

"Say it."

Trivia typed and pressed her thumb to the scroll. "Use of Semblances is not permitted on school grounds."

"Why?" Lady Beat asked.

"Not everyone has a Semblance and a lady must not make others feel inferior to her."

"And?" Lady Beat prodded.

"Semblances are a reflection of our true selves. Ladies do not reveal more than they need to."

"Very good. Now drop your illusion and go let Melanie and Miltia out of the closet."

Trivia released the illusion of her clothes. Lady Beat wrinkled her nose at the sight of her pink pajamas, the only things Trivia owned.

"Aren't you going to punish them?" Trivia asked. Again, the generated voice grated on her ears.

"Ladies don't tattle, Ms. Vanille. I am certain the Malachites have had ample opportunity to think over their actions, as I hope you will."

Trivia's mouth dropped open.

"Part of learning to be a lady is learning how to interact with others and settle disputes on your own. As long as you follow my rules, anything goes." Lady Beat smiled again, but this smile was more chilling. "But do try not to kill anyone. I don't like messy paperwork. Thank you, that's all. I'll see you in class."

As soon as Trivia unlocked the closet door, it burst open and Melanie and Miltia stormed out. Melanie laughed. "Look at her jammies, Miltia! They're so *twee*."

Miltia frowned and studied Trivia. "Where did her other uniform go?"

"Whatever. We've got to get to class, and she still has to change." Melanie smirked and sashayed away, her sister trailing behind like a shadow.

Trivia went into the closet and found her uniform on the floor. And on the sink. And on a few shelves. And inside a bucket.

The twins had torn it apart and scattered the pieces everywhere. Fortunately, the next class was sewing.

Trivia was aware of the attention from her classmates as soon as she sauntered into class in her pajamas. The other girls whispered to each other, wondering why Lady Beat wasn't punishing her for being out of uniform—unaware that she *was* being punished.

Trivia thought back to the conversation in Lady Beat's office. The headmistress clearly expected her students to fix their own problems without involving her. Breaking the rules meant she would have to get involved as a disciplinarian, which meant double the failure. What was Trivia expected to do?

As the old saying went, "You can't put the moon back together." At times you had to destroy something to make something even better in its place. When Mama had shattered Neopolitan outside their burning house, Trivia finally understood that *she* had been broken all along. Losing her friend was Trivia's first step toward putting herself back together and embracing her true, best self.

There was only one thing she could do now: Pick up the pieces and use them to make something new. So she tuned out her classmates and Lady Beat's voice and began stitching the cut fabric together. Rather than focus on repairing her uniform, she decided to get creative and make a new outfit: the kind of thing Neopolitan would wear. It had to be bold. It had to be eye-catching. It had to provide freedom of movement.

She shortened and hemmed the skirt, leaving cuts along the left and right seams for more mobility. She cut the sleeves of the jacket off at the elbow, and used the extra fabric salvaged from the skirt to lengthen the tailcoat. She deepened the neckline of the top and broadened the lapels, but she left the sleeves alone so they would extend beyond the jacket's sleeves.

Trivia hadn't been so caught up in her own little world in a long while, since she was little and making paper dolls and paper clothing to mix and match. Since she had used her Semblance for the first time to create a butterfly with one pink wing, one brown, with white spots all over—then sent it out through her bedroom window and watched it flutter away until she lost sight of it and let it go.

Finally, she was done. She attached the school pin to the lapel and looked up. She had been so absorbed in her work, in the act of destroying and creating, that it was now dark and she was the only one left in the classroom. Sewing class had ended hours ago, and no one had bothered to tell her. Or they weren't able to get her attention. She had missed dinner.

Trivia tried on her new uniform in the bathroom in front of the floor-length mirror, enjoying having it all to herself for once. Arguably she had perhaps done more damage to the uniform than the twins; there was now about 30 percent *less* of it. But it was a much less formal affair now. It felt comfortable and modern, streamlined and smart. It felt more like her. Wearing this, she almost, not quite, knew (or remembered?) who she was—not as a student or a daughter, but as Trivia Vanille.

She wrinkled her nose. Her name still felt like a coat that didn't fit right. She would need to tailor that, too.

She tilted her head and considered her reflection. Something was missing. Her hair shimmered as she flexed her Semblance to change her hair pink. *No, that's too much of the other girl.*

She combed her fingers through the hair on the right side, changing it back to brown so it matched the color of her right eye.

She smiled.

Yes, she thought. *There you are.* Finally seeing herself for the first time was like greeting an old friend. Someone she had missed for a long time. She winked at her reflection and the girl in the mirror winked back.

Trivia exited the bathroom and headed back to the dorm, moving softly like her old game of Tiptoe Tag. It was already after lights-out and she didn't want to be caught, considering she had already had one run-in with Lady Beat today. She was surprised to hear whispered voices coming down the corridor toward her.

She shielded herself behind an illusion of a potted fern just before Melanie and Miltia Malachite turned the corner and came into view. She thought they had sounded familiar. Their outfits were definitely not up to the dress code.

"It's been so long since we've been to a club," Miltia said. She was wearing a white sequined party top, white gloves, a black miniskirt, and red lace-up boots.

"I know! I so hate it here." Melanie's matching top and gloves were red, with the same black miniskirt and white boots.

"I'm not sure which I hate more, this school or Vale."

"I'm sure. It's this school and having to pretend—" Melanie stopped suddenly. She stared at the fern masking Trivia. "Hold up. Was that plant always there?"

"Who cares? Beat is always redecorating around here, 'Make it feel more like home.'"

Melanie squinted. Then she shrugged and they continued walking down the hall. "If she wanted it to feel more like home, she'd . . ." They moved out of earshot.

Trivia's research had only turned up one reference to the Malachite family of note: Lil' Miss Malachite, a crime boss in Mistral. But there had been no mention of her daughters, and why would a crime boss send her children to another Kingdom for school to learn how to become proper ladies? Still, it could explain why they were so bossy and acted like they owned everything and everyone. She wanted to find out what Miltia had been saying about pretending, so she dropped the illusion—a moving plant wouldn't fool anybody—and followed them quietly. She already noticed how much easier it was to move around in her new outfit.

"Just remember, this is business, not pleasure," Miltia said.

"I don't see why it can't be both."

"That's why the reminder."

It sure sounded like they were planning to go clubbing tonight, but that would require them to leave the school grounds, and that was the number one rule that guaranteed expulsion if you broke it.

Correction: If you were *caught* breaking it. If she got evidence that they had gone out, she could get *them* in trouble this time, maybe even get rid of them. Or it would be nice to have some evidence that she could hold over them.

It was time for Trivia to shift from defense to offense. She continued trailing after them at a safe distance, her Scroll set to silent mode and recording. The twins went down to the basement level, a twisty maze of corridors, conduits, and machinery. It was dark and warm down there, some pipes dripping with water, others spewing blasts of steam. Trivia repeated the turns they took so she'd be able to find her way again.

Right, Right, Straight, Left, Right, Left, Left, Right, Straight . . . And there was a steel door, marked ALARM WILL SOUND IF OPENED.

Miltia pushed the crash bar on the door and it opened. Trivia paused, listening. No alarm.

She waited for the girls to be far enough away that they wouldn't notice her exiting behind them. She pushed the crash bar and held it in as she eased the door open so it wouldn't make any noise. Before she closed it, she tested the handle from the outside; it was locked and she didn't have the key. She reached into a pocket— that's right, she had pockets now—and retrieved a small scrap of leftover fabric from her uniform. She jammed it into the strike plate hole so the door wouldn't be able to latch closed.

The secret exit had let her out into the garden behind the school, in the shade of a willow tree. She made a note of the spot and hurried after the Malachites.

As they went deeper into the city, she snapped some photos of them with her Scroll. The fact that they were off school grounds was incriminating enough. Of course she was, too, but she could claim she was only following them. Which she was.

As an added precaution, Trivia employed her Semblance to disguise herself as an elderly shopkeeper from a local bookshop. And it was a good thing, too. The twins stopped abruptly inside the entrance of a branch bank. Trivia continued walking past them, doing her best to look inconspicuous.

She rounded the next corner and waited there for a moment, out of sight, before peeking back around to see where they had gone. They had crossed the street and were knocking on the door of a place called the Harmony Club. A narrow slot slid open and Melanie started chatting with the person on the other side.

No way they're getting in there, she thought. They were obviously too young for a nightclub.

Her right eyebrow went way up when the door opened and Melanie and Miltia disappeared inside.

Trivia parked herself in the same doorway the Malachites had used and stepped back into the shadows, dropping her disguise. She had been practicing using her Semblance when no one was around to notice, and it no longer took a conscious effort to maintain an illusion once it was established. While it was active, she was always aware of it, like an itch at the back of her mind that she couldn't scratch. The longer she kept it running, the larger or more complicated the illusion, the more distracting it was.

She couldn't see through the mirrored glass of the windows, which reflected the glow of the streetlamps. There was only one way to find out what was happening inside.

She was tired of just watching. She wanted to be *doing* something.

Trivia was deciding on a disguise that would allow her to infiltrate the club when someone crashed through of one of the club's windows and thudded onto the sidewalk.

Trivia's eyes widened. The man groaned and got up, using a cane to pull himself onto his feet. He ran a gloved hand through his orange hair to shake out the broken glass and looked around on the ground until he found a brown bowler hat. He scooped it up with the hook of his cane and adjusted it on his head. He started to walk away, but he paused when Melanie and Miltia jumped out of the broken window.

"You're coming on a little strong. If you girls wanted to dance, all you had to do was ask. But please, you're going to have to take turns. I know you've never liked sharing."

Trivia smiled. This guy had a flair about him, keeping his calm after being thrown through a window.

The twins slowly moved in separate directions to flank him.

"The only thing we want to ask you is what you're doing here," Melanie said.

"I was just checking in on an old friend. But you're the last two people I'd expect to run into here. Isn't it way past your bedtime?"

"We'll sleep when you're dead," Melanie said.

"I'm surprised your dear mother let you come to Vale all by yourself. Well, tell her hi for me." The man gave them a jaunty wave and then started running down the street.

"Tell her yourself," Melanie said.

Trivia hit Record on her Scroll just in time to catch Melanie executing a series of cartwheels toward the man, the heels of her shoes glinting in the streetlights.

Blades hidden in her shoes, Trivia thought. *Great idea.*

The man spun and blocked her foot with his cane, the sharp point of her heel an inch from his throat. He twisted the cane, hooking her foot in it, and spun, propelling her toward Miltia, who was doing gymnastic flips toward him.

Miltia flipped over her sister and landed her feet in the man's chest, springing off him and somersaulting backward. He staggered back, a hand on his ribs.

"Cute," he said.

"Flattery's not going to work on me anymore," Miltia said.

"I was referring to your moves, not you."

Meanwhile, Melanie had recovered and ran toward the man. She dropped to her hands and spun her legs around in the air behind him.

Duck, Trivia thought.

The man did. Her heels just missed his head, knocking his hat to the ground again.

Trivia felt like she should be doing something—or maybe she just wanted to get in on the fight. But who should she help? She didn't know what their history was, but it seemed clear that the orange-haired man hadn't provoked this fight. He looked like he could hold his own, though.

But if Trivia helped Melanie and Miltia, maybe they would see her differently and stop bullying her. If they were grateful, maybe they could even become friends.

Trivia took a step forward.

Then the whole situation changed when three black cars rolled up and blocked the man's exit. Their doors opened and men spilled out. Large, angry men.

Trivia had the feeling she'd stumbled into something much bigger than even she could have imagined.

CHAPTER TWELVE

DOUBLE TROUBLE

As Roman enjoyed a delicious steak dinner with Honey Wine, a former colleague from Mistral, he had the distinct impression they were being watched.

He liked it that way.

These days, wherever he went, stares and whispers followed him. That was the price of fame. Roman's face was everywhere: on the news, on wanted posters, and online.

Naturally, Roman had ignored Hei Xiong's friendly advice and doubled down on his criminal activity over the last few months. He did make an effort to steer clear of places that did business with the Xiong family—no sense in asking for more trouble—but that left him with banks and convenience stores that were unprotected and unprepared. Law enforcement was a joke; they knew how to deal with a crime organization, but they had a harder time catching just one guy.

Roman had no underlings who could give him up, willingly or unwillingly. Other criminals had no incentive to cross him, and some of them even seemed to admire him. For now, Xiong seemed to be watching and waiting. He'd said his piece, and he clearly expected the police or Lil' Miss to take care of the problem sooner or later.

Meanwhile, Roman was carrying on the longest, most successful crime spree the city of Vale had ever seen. Even some of the public seemed ready to glorify him as one of the most exciting things to happen in Vale in a long time—as long as he wasn't causing them any direct harm, it gave them something to talk about. He was practically a folk hero.

"This is a great club, Honey. You're doing well for yourself," Roman said.

"Sweet of you to come by," she said. "When this hits the tabloids in the morning, I expect business will get even better. You didn't have to do that."

Roman flashed her a smile. "I probably owe you."

"You definitely do." She laughed.

When Roman had started working for Lil' Miss Malachite, she had reassigned Brick and Mortar's beat to him and Chameleon. Roman, after all, had pointed out they could be doing a better job and promised that he was the man to do it. So collecting the loyalty money from the Luck of the Mountains had become his job. Which was how he'd gotten to know Honey. She had turned out to be fascinating to talk to, and not just because of the sound of her voice. He wasn't surprised at all that she had worked her way out of the lower levels of Mistral and started a new life in Vale, with her own club.

"You ever think about the old days?" She leaned toward him. Her light skin sparkled with red Dust—a statement about how much money she had and her daredevil nature. A stray spark could blow her up and maybe her club with it. But it was also a striking fashion statement that looked good on her.

"Too often," he said.

"I'm the same," she said.

"When do you go on?" he asked, gesturing to the stage at the back of the club, currently featuring a live band. He had brought earplugs to muffle Honey's singing; as much as he loved the sound of her voice, he liked being in control of himself more.

"I don't do that anymore." She took a sip of water. "I'm trying to keep a low profile in Vale. But I wouldn't expect you to know anything about that."

Roman grinned.

"What are you doing, Roman?" she asked. "You sure drawing all this attention is smart? Every cop in the city is looking for you, and I know you've made plenty of enemies in the past."

He spread his hands as if to say, *Come on. Look who you're talking to.*

She folded her arms in front of her and lifted her eyebrows.

"It usually takes years to establish yourself as a crime boss. I'm just taking a shortcut," he said.

"Fake it 'til you make it."

"You know me too well."

She nodded, her glittery cheeks glinting distractingly. "I do, which is why I'm wondering why you're *really* here."

"Like I said, I heard about this place and I wanted to pay you a visit. We're friends, or so I thought."

Her face visibly relaxed. "Good, because if you're looking for a partner for one of your ridiculous schemes—I don't do *that* anymore, either." She glanced over his shoulder and groaned. "Uh-oh."

He wasn't completely surprised when he looked up and saw Melanie and Miltia Malachite walk in. He'd known he would have to reckon with Lil' Miss sooner or later if he was going to seize control of the Vale crime world. He guessed it was going to be sooner.

He stayed in his seat and kept eating and enjoying the live band, while keeping an eye on the twins. He hadn't seen them in some time, because Lil' Miss had sent them off to boarding school, he hadn't known where. He didn't think it was a coincidence that Xiong had noted more of a Spider presence in Vale, and now here were Lil' Miss's own daughters. Something was up.

The girls spoke with the hostess and she pointed toward Roman. Melanie nodded and they headed for his table.

So their presence here, tonight, wasn't a coincidence, either. Someone had tipped them off and they had come looking for him in particular.

Roman rose. "Ladies, fancy meet—"

Miltia punched him in the nose.

Roman staggered back and brought his hand up to his face.

"Oh, you're here for him." Honey stood up. "I've gotta get back to work. You break anything, you pay for it. Nice seeing you, Roman. Good luck." She bustled off.

Roman rubbed his nose. "You shouldn't have done that," he told Miltia.

"He's right, Mil. You should have done *this*." Melanie kicked the table and it flipped toward Roman's head. He ducked and it crashed behind him. His half-eaten steak landed at his feet. He picked up his cane and straightened up.

"They call me a crook, but what you just did to that prime rib is the real crime." At least the meal had been on the house.

Around them, customers shouted and scrambled to safety. They had all seen what Roman Torchwick could do on the news. And they'd just seen what Melanie and Miltia could do. They were all spoiled by complacency here; in Vale this was a disaster in the making. In Mistral, this was just a Tuesday.

Roman hopped back as Miltia took another swing at him. And another. She released a flurry of punches and kicks at him as he retreated and leaned his body to miss the blows.

"You're clearly working out some issues. I wish I could help."

Miltia paused.

"That's better. Now let's talk about this, shall we?"

Wait, where was Melanie?

He never saw where she had come from, but the next thing Roman knew, he was crashing through the window. He landed in the middle of the street. A car honked and veered around him.

It took Roman a second to catch his breath. He pulled himself up with his cane and looked around for his hat, shaking the glass out of his hair.

There. He hooked it with his cane, tapped the top, and put it back on.

Well, time to go. He started to walk away until he saw the twins climb through the broken window. The Malachites did not mess around.

They had a reputation to protect, and so did he. He didn't know if this was a personal vendetta or if they were carrying out their mother's hit on him.

"You're coming on a little strong. If you girls wanted to dance, all you had to do was ask. But please, you're going to have to take turns. I know you've never liked sharing," he said.

Melanie and Miltia moved apart to flank him, their movements perfectly synchronized. He'd had to endure their dance recitals when they were little. He'd clapped for them at gymnastic competitions. And now they were trying to do a number on him.

"The only thing we want to ask you is what you're doing here," Melanie said.

"I was just checking in on an old friend. But you're the last two people I'd expect to run into here. Isn't it way past your bedtime?"

"We'll sleep when you're dead," Melanie said.

"I'm surprised your dear mother let you come to Vale all by yourself. Well, tell her hi for me." Roman waved and then made a break for it.

"Tell her yourself." Melanie cartwheeled toward Roman. He heard the click of the blades as they slid from her shoes. Roman brought his cane up just in time to block her foot. Up close he saw the blade an inch from his throat.

He twisted his cane and hooked it around her foot, then he spun, pulling her around 360 degrees and releasing her to tumble toward Miltia as she backflipped toward him.

Miltia just cleared her sister and her feet hit Roman in the chest, knocking him back. She launched herself off him and twisted around midair to land on her feet.

Roman rubbed his chest. "Cute."

"Flattery's not going to work on me anymore," Miltia said.

"I was referring to your moves, not you."

Melanie reappeared on his left. She leaped into a handstand and spun her legs around behind him.

Roman dropped to his knees just in time, but his hat went flying off.

No more Mr. Nice Guy. He didn't want to hurt the little brats, despite everything, but he couldn't let them take him down.

He switched his cane to flare mode and started to get up—and that's when everything went sideways.

Unmarked cars screamed down the street toward him. He flinched when it looked like one might hit him, but it turned at the last moment and stopped. He looked behind him and found he was blocked on three sides. The doors opened and a dozen goons piled out onto the street, all of them training their guns on him.

They weren't dressed in Lil' Miss's colors, but he knew a Spider gang member when he saw one, even if their tattoos weren't visible.

He stood up, anyway. "So Lil' Miss is moving in on Vale. I guess that's the real reason she wants to shut me down."

Melanie laughed. "Get over yourself. You're not a threat; you're a distraction. But you're turning up the heat and jeopardizing her operation."

"What operation would that be?"

"Nice try. *Not*," Melanie said. "It might be hard for you to believe, but it doesn't concern you. You should be happy. You're going home."

Roman shook his head. "You'll have to kill me here, because there's no way I'm going back to Mistral."

"Did Mother specify dead or alive, Mel?" Miltia asked.

"Excellent point, Mil. She did not."

Roman was startled to see a little girl with pink-and-brown hair waving at him from the alleyway beyond the Malachite twins. Not waving—gesturing for him to come over to her.

Roman immediately returned his attention to the brats, hoping he hadn't tipped them off about the girl behind them. None of the other Spiders could see her because of their vantage point, and the fact that they were focused solely on him.

Roman loved alleyways. They were second nature to him. But unlike in Mistral, most of the alleys in Vale were dead ends. There was no reason to trust a stranger and he didn't see how going down there would help, but he also didn't have any other options. All he needed to do was get by Melanie and Miltia.

There was nothing for it. He was going all in.

Roman dashed toward Melanie and Miltia. Just as he reached them and they tried to grab him, he fired a flare straight downward and held on to his cane. The force of the explosion knocked the girls back and propelled Roman upward. He landed on his feet just in front of the alley and ran inside.

The girl was there. Up close he saw that her eyes were as mismatched as her hair: one was pink and one was brown. She was also older than her diminutive height suggested, maybe about the same age as the Malachite twins. She wore some kind of school uniform, a dark-blue business jacket and miniskirt with a silver pin on the lapel depicting three connected spirals.

He followed her down the alley until they came to a wall.

"Great." He looked up, but it wouldn't be easy to scale the walls. He was still boxed in, and the Spiders had him cornered.

"Dead end." Lots of bodies were discovered in one-way alleys like this in Mistral—eventually.

"How's this supposed to help?" he asked.

The girl closed her eyes and suddenly a brick wall appeared in front of them, blocking off the alleyway. Her pink hair flickered and faded to the same brown as the rest of her hair. When she opened her eyes, their color hadn't changed, though—only the expression behind them. She was surprised.

The wall was some kind of illusion, but when he reached out, it felt just as real as the wall at his back.

He heard muffled shouts from the other side. "Where is he? Where'd he go?"

"No way he could have gotten past us." Someone banged on the brick wall, but it held.

"I didn't think Torchwick had a Semblance," one of the Spiders said.

"Would be just like him to keep that under his hat."

Roman felt the top of his head. His hat was gone. The girl was looking Roman up and down, like she was trying to memorize every detail.

"Who are you? Is this—" He gestured at the wall.

She put a finger to her lips. She leaned her head toward the alleyway and cupped her hand around one ear. Listen.

Roman listened.

"There he is! He's getting away!"

Footsteps pounded back the way they'd come. Just then the fake brick wall disintegrated and disappeared.

Roman reached a hand out tentatively. The wall, which had just been solid a moment ago, was completely gone as if it had never been there.

"After him!" Melanie shrieked. A Spider car raced past the alley entrance with a squeal of tires.

"Get Torchwick!"

He snuck up to the edge of the alley and peered around the corner. The street was empty now except for the broken glass from the club window, and his hat—crushed in a tire track.

They'll pay for that, he thought.

He heard gunshots and looked down the road. The Spider cars were speeding down the street and gang members were shooting at—

Him. The running figure was far away, but it was dressed like him, right down to his cane.

He looked back at the girl who had saved his life. She was leaning against the wall, eyes closed, breathing fast. He didn't know how, but she was generating that duplicate Roman and leading them away. And it seemed like she wouldn't be able to keep the deception up forever.

Her eyes flew open and she looked right at him. She looked tired and afraid. She made a shooing motion with her hand.

Run.

Roman bowed to her and hurried away in the opposite direction.

He would live to die another day, but he was irritated. He didn't like owing anyone anything, especially not his life. He had to find out the identity of the stranger who had saved him. And he had an idea of how to find her.

CHAPTER THIRTEEN

NEW GIRL

When Trivia woke up, she wasn't quite sure if she had only dreamed about the night before or if it had really happened. She'd been so drained from creating two illusions at once, the wall being the largest she had ever attempted, and the duplicate of Torchwick the first she'd ever sustained long distance. She was sure she had left his attackers even more confused when he ultimately faded away before their eyes, she thought with a grin.

Torchwick. She had no idea who he was, or why she'd saved him. Maybe it was just because he had seemed so confident—arrogant even—despite being outmatched and outnumbered. Except for that one moment, when he was down and doubt flickered over his face for just a split second, replaced almost immediately by determination. Fair bet he was planning to go down fighting.

He was used to pretending and hiding his true self behind that hat and suit and ponytail. She knew what that was like.

Trivia yawned and stretched and opened her eyes. For the first time in months, she wasn't dreading the day. Now that she knew that the Malachite girls were up to something, she couldn't wait to find out their secret.

She glanced at her alarm clock and jumped out of bed.

I'm late!

She was also still dressed in her uniform, since she had snuck back in late and collapsed into bed. So she grabbed her bag and ran. She slowed down only when she reached the classroom so she could walk in calmly as though she'd planned to be late.

Everyone turned to look at her. Several girls gasped and stared.

What? Trivia looked around a little perplexed. It wasn't that shocking that she was so late.

"What did she do to her uniform?" some of the girls whispered.

Oh, that. Trivia had forgotten that she'd modified her uniform after Melanie and Miltia's little prank. She spotted them in their usual seats at the back of the room. They looked as tired as she felt, and annoyed—they were probably not too pleased that Torchwick had slipped through their fingers. But they didn't know it was because of Trivia. Trivia winked at them, and they looked at each other in surprise.

"What did she do to her *hair*?" another girl said.

Trivia reached up and felt her hair, worried someone had cut it in her sleep. Another bully had tried that shortly after Trivia had arrived at the school, but Trivia had woken up just in time, grabbed the shears, and slashed the girl's cheek with them. The other girls started making fun of her, calling her Scarface, and she hadn't bothered Trivia again.

Trivia's hair was all there, but when she tugged on it, she noticed that the right side was pink again. This time, her Semblance had done it unconsciously once her Aura had recovered enough. She smiled.

Lady Beat clapped her hands. "That's enough, girls. Trivia,

thank you for joining us. You're late. Please see me after class. Now take your seat."

Trivia nodded and hurried to her desk.

Today's class was diction, which normally Trivia found excruciating, but Lady Beat wouldn't allow her to sit it out. She said it would do her good to follow along with the other girls, anyway, in case she was able to speak one day, or could communicate by mouthing the words. She also made Trivia use the voice synthesis on her Scroll when it was her turn, which just seemed unnecessarily cruel.

But that gave Trivia an excuse to use her Scroll in class, which was normally off-limits. First she used the selfie camera to get a look at her hair.

It seemed Neopolitan was here to stay. She had tried to summon her friend many times since the night of the fire, but after seeing her mother shatter her like that she just couldn't make her appear—until now. She had realized that Neo was really just another aspect of herself, but this made it feel, well . . . real. She twirled a finger around a lock of pink hair.

She caught Melanie watching her. She pulled down her eyelid and stuck out her tongue.

"Melanie," Lady Beat said.

Melanie looked surprised, then she recited from the text on her Scroll, "The gruesome Grimm grew greedy. Get that greedy gruesome Grimm, Gregory. Go, Gregory, go. The greedy gruesome Grimm gored Gregory. Good-bye, Gregory, good-bye. The gory, greedy Grimm gave a gruesome grin."

Trivia smiled and went back to her own Scroll. She started by looking up Torchwick. She hadn't expected to find much, but his picture showed up immediately along with a number of articles and video clips. Roman Torchwick.

A bank robber? Trivia thought excitedly. *I rescued a bank robber.*

Every article said the same thing about him: "Armed and dangerous." "Unstable." "Violent."

People have said worse about me, Trivia thought. But no one had seen him like she had, afraid and vulnerable.

There was a reward out for any tips that led to his arrest in Vale. There was also a bounty on his head in the Kingdom of Mistral, posted on all the Huntsmen job boards.

Trivia started to search for "spiders" and "Malachite" when a shadow appeared on her screen and Lady Beat said, "Trivia."

Trivia quickly swiped away from the search engine, accidentally pressing Play on her voice app. It blasted the last line she had typed, "Aren't you going to punish them?"

She glanced at Melanie and Miltia while giggles broke out. The twins narrowed their eyes at her.

Lady Beat put her hand on Trivia's shoulder and squeezed. "After class," she reminded her.

Trivia swallowed. Had Lady Beat seen Torchwick's picture on her screen? Trivia felt oddly embarrassed, but she didn't know why. He was currently public enemy number one, so it would make sense for him to come across her news feeds—only she preferred reading fiction to the news. Which was why she'd never heard of him before.

If she had recognized Torchwick, would she have still saved him?

Of course. It was enough that Melanie and Miltia were interested in him. And that made Trivia interested in them. According to her search, their mother owned a tavern in lower Mistral, but given the conversation from last night, she gathered that wasn't the extent of her entrepreneurship. Torchwick had seemed surprised to find them in Vale. They knew each other, so the Malachite girls were probably criminals, too. If they were in Vale, they were up to something—and she was willing to bet Lady Browning's Preparatory Academy for Girls was somehow involved.

At the end of class, Trivia waited for the rest of the students to file out, which they did very slowly because they all wanted to see what kind of trouble she was in.

"Close the door and come here, Ms. Vanille," Lady Beat said.

Trivia followed her orders and stood in front of Lady Beat's desk. The woman steepled her fingers and looked her over.

"You've changed. And I'm not referring to your new hairstyle or your suit, although, *obviously*." Lady Beat rose and walked around Trivia. "You look good. Contrary to popular belief, the clothes do not make the woman. But they can reveal so much about a person. Do you know why we have a uniform at this school?"

Trivia shook her head.

"You say no, but your face says otherwise. Go on, you can type it if you must."

Trivia typed out her answer. Before she could play it aloud on her Scroll, Lady Beat looked over her shoulder and read it aloud: "To discourage individualism.

"I can see why you would think that, but it's actually the opposite.

The rules say you must wear the uniform, but nowhere does it say you cannot modify the uniform. Nor are there strict guidelines on how it should be worn, length, and so on. It is very rare for a student to get creative with her uniform; the last one who did so now has her own fashion label." Lady Beat smiled. "But your design is better."

She returned to her desk. "Everyone wears the same outfit here to make it easier to see *how* they wear it. How comfortable are they in it? How do they maintain it? Can they still express themselves? Similarly, all students participate in the same classes here, so I can better evaluate their strengths and their weaknesses. Do you understand?"

Trivia frowned. Sort of. It sounded like it was all some kind of test—a control experiment. But she thought controlling them was the whole point. The school was supposed to change them, and you don't do that in an experiment.

So you can fix us? Trivia typed. She held up her screen, her hand trembling slightly.

Lady Beat read her screen. Tears came to her eyes. "My dear, there's nothing to fix. You aren't broken. None of you are."

Trivia drew in a breath. She suspected her parents thought otherwise.

"It saddens me that you think that. I blame your parents."

Trivia looked at her sharply.

"I blame society." Lady Beat gestured to the symbol on the wall behind her, the same on the gold pin she wore. "No one ever asks what this means. Why you wear it every day. Three spiral shapes connected at their center. We are ruled by thirds. In fashion, we combine no more than three colors. Our personalities are defined by the id, the ego, and the superego. We have our best instincts, our worst impulses, and the expectations of society—always warring, vying for control. But our goal, is harmony." She gestured to the symbol. "Balance."

She sat down. "If you let one aspect dominate, or suppress another, things can spiral out of control. When you remove one from the others, you have chaos; but bring them all together and you have something . . ." She leaned back and smiled at Trivia. "Something beautiful."

Trivia's mind was spiraling now. She had thought she was going to be in trouble, because every time she had done something unexpected, something that strayed from what her parents wanted, she had been punished for it. No place had seemed to have more rules than Lady Browning's Preparatory Academy for Girls, but individuality—breaking the rules, was what Lady Beat wanted?

Trivia threw up her hands in confusion. **I thought we were supposed to follow the rules, but you want us to break them?**

"I wanted you to learn the rules and think about how to bend them. If you must break them, don't get caught. We are expected to follow the rules, but when we do, we aren't rewarded—we are simply expected to follow more rules. Never question them. Never try to change them." Lady Beat clapped her hands. "No, thank you. If you want to get ahead in life, all you need to do is *appear* to follow the rules. As you know better than anyone, appearances can be deceiving."

Trivia tilted her head. *Why are you telling me this?*

"I want to apologize to you, Ms. Vanille. I underestimated you, and because of that, I failed you. You're bored here, aren't you?"

Completely. Trivia shook her head.

Lady Beat winked. "You're a natural at deception. And I should have seen it sooner. Your talents are being wasted, and so I am inviting you to join the advanced curriculum at the school."

Trivia's eyebrows shot up.

"Did you think this was all it was? Posture and diction? Girls usually aren't ready for the real lessons until their second or third year, if they are ever deemed worthy. But you, I think, are a special case. With the proper training, you could be spectacular. I'm sure you have—"

Trivia flashed her screen at Lady Beat. **YES.**

"No questions?"

Trivia shook her head. She was practically jumping up and down with excitement.

"There is one thing I need from you, however. A sign that you are ready to commit yourself completely to becoming the best *you* you can be."

Trivia frowned.

"You seem to have taken an interest in Roman Torchwick. He is a very dangerous criminal, and I have reason to believe he endangers the very existence of this school."

How does she know about that? Trivia thought, immediately wary. **You want me to stay away from him.**

"On the contrary. I want you to find out what he's planning. If we could help bring him to justice for his crimes, we would be doing a good deed—and get some positive coverage of our mission here."

Trivia bit her lip. It sounded like Lady Beat was giving her an assignment and the promise of more freedom, and all she had to do was keep tabs on Torchwick and get closer to him. Which she had wanted to do, anyway.

Trivia nodded.

"Please answer, with your voice app this time. Trivia Vanille, will you help me capture Roman Torchwick?"

Trivia typed her response slowly. She pressed Play. "You can count on me."

"I know I can. Very well. Go collect your things."

Trivia raised an eyebrow.

"You're moving to your own room."

Just as quickly as Trivia's life had turned upside down when her parents dumped her at the school, her fortunes had changed again, only this time for the better.

She was now living in a second-floor dorm room, which she had all to herself, though it had a bunk bed designed for two students. It was a far cry from the room she'd had at home, but far better than sharing a space with nineteen other girls. She even had a private bathroom again.

She was also closer to the Malachite girls, who lived on the opposite end of the hall. And her window made it even easier for her to sneak out.

Her class schedule now included fascinating lessons like Introduction to Self-Defense, Social Engineering, The Art of Escape, Computer Science, and Fencing (though at this point she didn't know if that meant fighting with swords or selling stolen goods—either way, she was up for it).

It was almost too good to be true, she thought as she leaped lightly from her window to the tree right outside it. She crouched on a sturdy branch and looked back at the school.

What if it *was* too good to be true?

Was she jeopardizing her new standing at the school by sneaking out again? Now that she knew it had all been a kind of test to see what she would do, was she still being scrutinized? If so, she could actually get into trouble by betraying Lady Beat's trust.

Or, if she didn't do whatever she wanted, without drawing attention to herself, *that* might be failing.

Trivia put her hands to the sides of her head and opened her mouth in a silent scream. They really knew how to mess with your mind here.

Lady Beat had spoken about balance. Trivia stood and raised one foot, standing on the other. It was shaky at first, but as she thought about what she wanted, and why she was sneaking out, she felt more in balance and she stood up straight. She had Lady Beat's expectations in mind, her parents' expectations, and then her own interests. Trivia had always pushed those down, stamped them out. She'd let Neopolitan take the risks and take the blame.

But the pink-haired girl had really been a part of her all along, a part that she hadn't been ready, or able, or allowed to accept. It was time to let her out to play.

Trivia hopped down to a lower branch and then did a somersault to the ground. She clapped for herself and skipped away toward the shops.

She went shoplifting first. She needed pink hair dye, so she wouldn't have to keep her Semblance active all the time to maintain her new look. She also needed some things to aid her in espionage and in her search for Roman Torchwick: a burner Scroll, a new computer, a lock-picking kit, and assorted spy gadgets. (You could find anything in the city.) Some things for fun: books and video games, because you had to treat yourself sometimes, and a few new outfits and accessories, including a gift for someone special. When the shops started to close, she headed back to the school. After a couple of blocks, she realized someone was following her. The hairs on the back of her neck rose and her muscles tensed.

Try to give them the slip? Hide? That's what the old Trivia would have done, but she didn't want to run anymore. If someone was interested in what she was doing, then she was interested in what they were doing.

She turned and scanned the street. Not many people out, and not many places to hide, but she found the most likely spot: the shadowed entryway of a shuttered noodle shop. She stomped toward it.

As she reached it, a figure in a black hooded sweatshirt, black pants, and expensive black leather shoes stepped onto the street in front of her.

Her heart raced. She wondered if she'd done the wrong thing after all. But she calmed down a moment later. His face was obscured, but she recognized his smirk. That voice.

"Hey, kid," Roman Torchwick said.

Trivia narrowed her eyes. She drew back her right arm and swung with all her might, whacking him in the face with her shopping bags. He staggered over and nearly fell onto the street, but he caught himself on a lamppost. He put up his hands—he was unarmed. He backed away.

"Whoa! Sorry for the surprise there. It's me." He lowered his hood. With his tousled orange hair, dressed like a street punk, he didn't look much older than her. In fact, he was kind of cute.

Come on, Trivia. She looked away with a scowl and crossed her arms. Her expression showed how much she was annoyed at herself as well as him.

"No? Thought you'd be happier to see me . . ." He shook his head. "Not sure why."

She rolled her eyes. He didn't get it.

He snapped his fingers. "Hold on. You don't like being called 'kid.'"

Trivia was astonished.

He grinned. "Knew it. That's fair. I apologize." He bowed with his hands pressed together. "My name is Roman." He lowered his voice and looked around uneasily. "Roman Torchwick."

Duh.

He put his hand behind his head and laughed. "Which of course you know. I mean, not 'of course.' Not to make it sound like I'm famous or anything . . ."

Trivia smiled. Sometimes it was better to not talk, because you could end up embarrassing yourself. But there was something endearing about seeing this tough guy unsure about himself, presumably a feeling he wasn't all that familiar with.

And it was awesome that it was her putting him on such shaky ground.

"So, what should I call you?" he asked.

Trivia considered for a moment. Then she pulled out her Scroll and typed her name. She stared at it for a moment.

"You don't have to tell me if you don't want to," Roman said. "Naturally. Not that you need my permission. I'm just saying."

Trivia deleted her name and started over. She showed him the screen.

"Nice to meet you, Neopolitan," he said.

She had given Neo's name because her own would have been giving away too much information, but in a way it was an even more personal thing to share. When she heard Roman say it aloud, it felt right.

It felt real.

It felt like *her*.

She was making a fresh start at life, finally becoming the person she had always wanted to be. And she couldn't do that if she continued thinking of herself as Trivia. So from now on she would be Neopolitan.

"Thank you again for the assist the other night," Roman said.

She shrugged nonchalantly. He didn't ask about why she wasn't talking. That was . . . nice. She typed a question.

Why were you following me?

"That's a much bigger question than you think. But you should also be wondering, how did I find you? You don't think I was just randomly walking the streets hoping I'd run into you, did you?"

She put a finger on her cheek thoughtfully. *Good point.*

How *had* he found her? She was a little disappointed. She'd been looking forward to the challenge of tracking him down and proving herself—but this certainly helped her fulfill her end of the bargain with Lady Beat.

He pulled his hood back up. "What do you say we get out of the open and have a private chat? Come on, I'll buy you a drink."

He turned and walked down the street, without waiting for her answer, without looking back to see if she was coming.

Neopolitan picked up her bags and followed Roman.

CHAPTER FOURTEEN

TEA FOR TWO

From the way Neopolitan delicately sipped her tea and ate her finger sandwiches, Roman could tell she had been taught good manners, or more likely had them inflicted on her.

The Laughing Dog was his favorite tea room in Vale. It was modeled after Mistrali tea rooms, right down to the paper folding screens around the booths to provide some measure of privacy.

"You want to know how I found you," Roman said.

Neopolitan sat back and swept a hand toward him, inviting him to go ahead.

"It was that pin you're wearing." Roman stuffed a whole finger sandwich into his mouth. None of that refined nibbling for him. If you didn't know where or when your next meal was coming, you didn't waste time eating. Of course he normally wouldn't be eating in a tea shop, but that was exactly why he was here—because no one would think to look for Roman Torchwick in a tea shop, either.

It certainly wasn't because he'd wanted to impress her or anything.

Get it together, Roman, he thought. He wasn't acting like himself.

It felt important somehow, this meeting. He knew that she could see right through him, so he didn't feel like he needed to pretend with her. And she wouldn't respect him if he tried. She also didn't seem afraid of him, or to want anything from him.

That was kind of refreshing, really.

Neopolitan looked down at the pin on her lapel. She traced one of the swirls with a distant look in her eyes.

"I looked it up. I wasn't expecting to get quite so many hits. That triple spiral, it's kind of a symbol for ladies in high society. A badge or whatever." Roman flipped through his Scroll and showed her photos from the Vale society pages and profiles of women in business. Many of them wore a matching pin, but in gold. "And then there's your uniform, though you've updated it some. It wasn't hard to connect you with Lady Browning's Preparatory Academy for Girls."

Roman slurped his tea. Neopolitan scrunched up her face.

"So that's lesson number one," he went on. "Learn to disguise yourself better if you're going to commit a crime."

She gave a lopsided grin. A pink shimmer traveled down her from her head, transforming her into a perfect copy of Roman, the way he'd been dressed last night, complete with the hat he'd lost.

His mouth fell open, and Neopolitan's mouth mirrored the action, showing him just how astonished he was.

He laughed. "Well, you've passed the first lesson already. You're a quick study."

Roman had always looked down on Semblances, and not because he didn't have one, as far as he knew. Most of the ones he'd encountered were only good in combat, and while Roman could hold his own in a fight—usually—he would much rather rely on his intellect, charm, and roguish good looks to get what he wanted. He didn't mind cheating, as long as he did it fair and square.

But an ability like Neopolitan's . . . That opened up a whole world of possibilities. She had already demonstrated how handy it was in last night's escape, and it had some good strategic value as well. The heists he could pull off with a power like that! The information he could control. The cons he could come up with.

"I'm impressed," he said.

Neopolitan blushed—still wearing his face. That was sure unnerving.

"And I'm honored. I rather expect you don't go showing off to just anyone."

She shook her head. She pointed at Roman, then held up one finger. She counted off two, three, four.

"Only a few people know about it. That's good. Just be careful who you trust. People might try to use you."

She raised an eyebrow.

So him, he assumed her parents—who was the fourth person who knew about her Semblance? Sister? Best friend? Significant other? Neopolitan seemed to be a loner like Roman—he recognized a kindred spirit in her. So maybe it was the school's headmistress, Lady Beatrix Browning.

Why had Neopolitan decided to risk exposing her Semblance and herself by using it to save a complete stranger last night?

Neopolitan's form shimmered and she was now Roman dressed as he was now with his black hoodie. She covered her head with her hood and looked shiftily back and forth.

"That's right. I'm laying low, too. I've discovered that the downside to being so recognizable is that you're easier to find when people come looking for you."

She changed into Melanie Malachite, nailing the girl's disaffected expression perfectly. "Melanie" was dressed in a school uniform similar to Neopolitan's.

"She goes to your school? So that's why you happened to be there when things went down."

Neopolitan nodded. She typed: **How do you know the Malachites?**

Roman sighed. "That is a long story."

Neopolitan lifted the teapot and refilled his cup and then her own.

"All right, then." So he told her about his mother abandoning him as a child in Wind Path. About living on the streets, stealing to survive, and joining Lil' Miss Malachite's organization as a step toward bigger and better things.

By the time he was finished, their second pot of tea was empty and Neopolitan had finally had her fill of sandwiches and cakes.

"I've never told anyone all that before," Roman said. Then again, he hadn't known anyone who would have cared. "But I'm nothing special. Lots of people in Mistral have a story like that. Or worse. You don't fall into a life of crime when you grow up having everything."

Neopolitan cupped her chin with her hand and looked pensive.

"Present company excepted. But you aren't a hardened criminal yet and I wouldn't recommend it."

She shook her head and frowned.

"I mean, sure, you get to do whatever you want. No one tells you what to do." He yawned. "You can stay up as late as you like."

He winked. "As long as you don't get caught. Or mixed up with someone like Lil' Miss."

He gestured to her shopping bags. "So what is all that stuff, anyway?"

She showed him some of the things she'd picked up. "Hair dye? You going to do the other half, too?"

She smiled and ran her hand through the pink side of her hair. It turned its natural dark brown.

"You tried it out and decided to make it permanent." She nodded. "It suits you. I like your eyes, too."

She smiled and continued showing off the rest of her haul.

"Looks like you're planning something big. What are you messing around with lock picks for?"

She hesitated and then reached for her Scroll. She typed a response quickly.

Expanding my horizons.

He grinned. "Well, I can certainly help with that. I'd be happy to show you the ropes."

Neopolitan clapped.

He leaned in a bit and lowered his voice. "But listen, how would you like to do some real spy stuff?"

She leaned forward eagerly.

"I've heard rumors that Lil' Miss is challenging the Vale crime bosses—expanding *her* horizons, if you know what I mean. If her daughters are at your school, that can't be a coincidence . . . I'm thinking they're involved somehow. Would you mind snooping around the academy a little?"

She looked down at the table, biting her lip. He'd expected her to jump at the opportunity. There certainly seemed to be no love lost between her and Melanie and Miltia.

He was surprised when she shook her head.

"No." He leaned back in his seat. "You won't help me. Mind if I ask why?"

She typed a response more slowly and seemed reluctant to show him the screen.

I can't risk getting kicked out.

Roman laughed. "You don't want to miss school. Okay." He held up a hand. "Okay. You know, it's better that way. You're right—you shouldn't hang around with me. You'll just get into trouble and regret it one day. Why ruin a good thing, right?"

Neopolitan looked upset. She put her hands together and bowed her head in apology.

"Don't worry. It's fine. Hey, I'm still grateful, and I still owe you for your help. So if you ever need me, just say the word."

She nodded. Then her face brightened and she picked up a bag. She handed it to Roman.

"I already have a lock-picking kit . . ." He opened the bag. Inside was a new bowler hat.

"You stole this for me? You shouldn't have." He examined it. "It's exactly like my old one."

She shook her head. She pointed at a red feather sticking from the hatband.

He laughed. "Okay, you're right—this is better than my old one."

No one had ever given him a gift before, either. What were you supposed to say when someone did something nice for you? "Well. Thanks."

He patted his belly. "We should probably get out of here now. You head for the bathroom and sneak out the back, and I'll slip out the front when the waitress's back is turned."

Neopolitan pursed her lips. She waved her hand in the negative.

"What do you mean 'no'?"

Neopolitan stood, gathered her bags, and tossed a wad of bills on the table. Then she walked out.

Roman picked up the money. It felt real enough. He followed Neopolitan out, glancing behind him to see that the cash was still there. The waitress waved to him and wished them a good night.

Neopolitan yanked him out the door and closed it softly behind her.

"Was that real money?" he asked.

She shook her head.

"So it's going to disappear eventually?"

She nodded.

"As soon as she puts it in the register?"

Neopolitan put her finger on her nose.

"Wow. That's messed up. But I like the way you work."

He didn't quite get how her Semblance worked, but it sure could come in handy.

"And I think we might actually work well together. So if you change your mind about that favor I asked you for, look me up. See you around." Roman popped his new hat on and started to walk away.

Neopolitan whistled. He turned. She spread her hands and shrugged.

"Don't want to make it too easy on you." He winked. "I found you. Let's see if you can find me."

He tipped his hat and walked away.

CHAPTER FIFTEEN

FIGHT AND FLIGHT

Neopolitan circled Manda Rin slowly, watching the way the Huntress moved, looking for a weakness. The older woman had three advantages over her: She was much bigger and stronger. She had a fire sword. And Neo couldn't use her Semblance at school, especially in front of her entire self-defense class.

Neo hefted her wooden training sword. She didn't like the heavy weapon; it was throwing off her balance. She wanted something lighter to fight with, like Roman Torchwick's cane. A weapon that matched her personality.

"Any day now," Rin said.

Neo blew her bangs out of her eyes and rushed toward the instructor, swinging the sword. Rin parried easily with her own sword and lunged for Neo. Neo hopped up lightly onto the broad blade. Rin tried to shake her off. Neo vaulted away just as the Huntress activated the flames, somersaulting over the Huntress. She planned to land behind her and whack her with her sword, but Rin turned and kicked high while Neo was still in the air. The Huntress's foot connected with Neo's stomach, knocking the wind out of her and knocking her clear across the room.

Neo jumped up instantly, spinning the wooden sword like a baton, a fierce scowl on her face.

"Good try, new girl," Rin said. "You're fast and clever, both excellent qualities in a fight. Does anyone know what Trivia did wrong?"

Neo blinked at the use of her old name. Of course she hadn't told anyone to start calling her Neopolitan, but she already felt disconnected from her former life. She lowered the sword and walked back to the arena.

"She tried to punch above her weight," Melanie Malachite said.

"Not quite. A person Trivia's size could very easily get the best of me. Her size can actually be an asset, especially if it makes others underestimate her," Rin said.

"She zigged when she should have zagged," Laurel said. The class laughed, but not in a mean-spirited way. Neo was there for a reason, like all of them, and she deserved some respect for volunteering to go up against the teacher first. And they all knew they would be next and might not fare any better.

"That's a bit closer," Rin said. "She had a good strategy, but you need to have at least three plans for every movement in every fight. Do you attack? Do you defend? Do you dodge? And you need to keep your eyes on your opponent, read what they're going to do and in that split second react appropriately. Naturally, if they're a good fighter, they're doing the same thing you are." She sheathed her weapon. "In some ways it's more like a dance than a fight. And you need to pick up on the subtle cues your partner gives you by constantly studying their body language, and not allowing yourself to be misdirected or distracted."

Rin bowed to Neo and Neo returned the gesture.

"I know this isn't a combat school, but by the time we're done here, you will be as skilled as any Huntress in Remnant." Rin tapped the gold triskelion pinned over her breast. "I was a student here just like you, so I know it's possible."

"But what's the point?" another girl asked. "I don't like fighting."

"Not fighting is a privilege. Entrusting your safety to people like me is a privilege." Rin looked at her sword.

"You may not feel like the Grimm are much of a threat here in the city, but you never know what they're capable of. I've seen some things in the field you would not believe. Grimm who can learn and adapt to fight humans and Faunus better. As if they weren't tough enough."

"Not to mention other people," Melanie said.

"True. You also need to be prepared to defend yourself against others." Rin sheathed her weapon. "And willing to do whatever it takes to get what you want."

Neo's eyes rounded. She didn't think that sounded like something a Huntress would say.

"You're surprised? In my time in the field, I've learned that the most important thing to keeping order is showing strength. Respect isn't enough to keep people safe—you need their admiration. And they need to be more afraid of the alternative than they are of you. Not everyone is able to master that. And fewer still are ready to accept it. Are you?"

Neo nodded. She saw Melanie and Miltia look at her and put their heads together.

After class, on the way to the lunchroom, the sisters flanked her in the hall. Neo steeled herself for another fight.

"We were wrong about you, Vanille. Maybe you do have what it takes to be here," Melanie said.

"You're sitting with us today," Miltia said.

Neo hesitated and then nodded, as though that sounded okay with her.

The school had been a nightmare before, but now it was a dream come true. The problem was, it was someone else's dream. She had never wanted to be accepted by the popular girls—she had only wanted to be accepted by *someone*. Now she was sitting at Melanie and Miltia's table, and she should be happy that she wasn't alone and no one was making fun of her.

What she really wanted to do was embarrass the twins in front of the whole school and take revenge on all the bullies who had been picking on Neo since she'd arrived. But she needed to pretend to want to be their friend to get information that would convince Roman she was on his side. And she needed to keep Roman on the hook so Lady Beat would continue to trust her and leave her free to do what she wanted.

Double-dealing was exhausting, but it gave her a thrill, too.

"Trivia, what does your family do, exactly?" Miltia asked. "I know your daddy's rich or you wouldn't be here."

"You live in that big mansion on the hill, right?" Melanie asked.

Not anymore, Neo typed. She held up her Scroll to show the words backward so they could see it on the other side of the display. It was like she had her own subtitles, translating what she was really thinking into what they wanted to hear.

"Your dad's well connected, though."

I guess. He works out business contracts for the city.

"We know how important the people behind the scenes are. That's why Lil' Miss always replaces them with her own people first thing."

Neo feigned ignorance. **Who?**

"Lil' Miss is our mother. She runs things in Mistral," Melanie said.

"I'm sure she'd like to meet your father," Miltia said.

Neo shook her head.

"Why not? Is he already working for someone else?"

It's not that. He wouldn't be interested. He's big on RULES. Neo rolled her eyes. She gestured around her. Why else did they think she was there?

"Everyone has their price. Even you." Melanie smiled, but in a mean way.

Neo looked down. She was right, though, wasn't she? But the arrangement she had was pretty victimless. She was just sharing information, and since she was playing both Roman and Lady Beat, it would all even out in the end. The only thing that mattered was Neo coming out ahead, for the first time in her life.

"Hey, we're going clubbing tonight! You should come, too, Vanille," Miltia said.

Neo's eyes went round. **You're sneaking off campus?**

"I wouldn't call it sneaking, since we pretty much—"

"Beat gave us a special assignment," Melanie cut in quickly. "It comes with some privileges."

The confusion on Neo's face was real. The twins had gone after Roman the other night. She had thought they'd just happened to run into him, but what if they'd known where to find him, and Lady Beat had sent them after him? In that case, it was a good thing Neo didn't try to turn them in for leaving school after all. It seemed that Lady Beat had given them the same deal Neo had gotten. So they were effectively competing against each other.

That would be just like Lady Beat, to play them off one another and give them all the same goal, to improve her chances of success. If Melanie and Miltia brought in Roman, where would that leave Neo? No wonder they were suddenly welcoming her. She had to make sure she got to Roman first, stayed close, and protected him from them if she had to.

Miltia flicked a chicken nugget at Scarface the next table over with a bored look on her face. Just yesterday, Neo probably would have been the unlucky target of her childish bullying.

"So it's settled. You're in. You can borrow one of my outfits," Melanie said.

Neo shook her head.

"Oh, you have other plans?"

Neo shrugged. She put her hands together in front of her, palms up, and looked down at them.

"I don't get it," Miltia said.

"Use your words," Melanie said exasperatedly.

Neo raised an eyebrow and typed. **Catching up on reading tonight.**

"Really? That's a snorefest."

Neo shrugged. **Another time. Thanks!** She smiled.

"Whatever," Melanie said.

Neo did have "homework" to catch up on, but she was fairly certain it would be anything but boring. In fact, she was really looking forward to it.

CHAPTER SIXTEEN

PARTNERS IN CRIME

Someone knocked on Roman's door. He checked the security camera by his door, and his blood ran cold for a moment.

Lil' Miss Malachite was standing on the other side.

He grabbed his cane from the umbrella stand and prepared himself to face his old boss.

"You're in control here," Roman muttered to himself. "She's on your turf this time."

The more he looked at her image on the screen, the more she looked slightly . . . off. She was shorter, for one thing, and her mole was under her left eye for another. Her face was five years younger than she'd appeared when they'd met. So unless she'd had a lot of work done lately—and she had never been that caught up about her appearance—this was an impostor.

Roman opened the door. "Hello, Neopolitan," he said.

Lil' Miss looked disappointed. He saw the familiar pink shimmering lights as Neopolitan dropped her disguise and trudged into the apartment, carrying a parasol over one shoulder and a sour expression. He closed the door behind her.

She looked back at him, a question on her face.

"Well, first, Lil' Miss Malachite wouldn't knock on the door—she would knock it down," he said.

Neopolitan slapped her hand against her forehead.

"Second, she wouldn't be alone. She always has a bodyguard with her. I know, because it was me for a while. I don't think she even needs one, but it helps make people underestimate her."

Neopolitan nodded. She'd remembered that part of his story.

"Third, Lil' Miss never leaves Mistral. Which is what makes it so strange that she'd be making a move on Vale. 'Better to be a strong queen than a weak emperor,' she used to say. She only trusts her people so far—even her own daughters. So she wouldn't leave things up to others unless she could somehow supervise operations closely." He paused. "You also must have found an old photo of Lil' Miss. My advice: Only try to impersonate people you've seen in real life."

She sighed.

"But it was a good effort. Sure surprised me at first."

That cheered her up enough to take an interest in his apartment. She started strolling around with her hands clasped behind her, studying every object like it was part of a museum exhibit.

"Mind if I ask *you* a question?" he asked.

She tossed a hand back behind her. *Go ahead.*

"How did you find me?" Honestly, he hadn't expected to ever meet Neopolitan again after she'd turned down his request for her help, or he never would have issued a challenge he didn't think she could complete. For all his efforts to get his name out there in the criminal underworld, you couldn't just look Roman Torchwick up in the phone book. The only reason Hei Xiong's men had been able to find him was because he had wanted them to.

He supposed he had wanted Neopolitan to find him, too, but he hadn't made it easy for her. Or had he?

Neopolitan gave him a sly smile. He waited, wondering if she was going to reveal her secrets. Then she reached up to the side of her head and plucked a small feather out of midair. She blew it toward him and it disintegrated into glowing pink particles before it reached his face.

A feather?

Roman squinted and took off his hat. The hat Neopolitan had given him at the tea shop. He had thought the feather was just for decoration, but . . . He pulled it out and held it up to his eye.

The feather shaft was made of a thin metal wire and there was a tiny computer chip at its base.

"A transponder?" He looked at Neopolitan in awe. She held up her Scroll so he could see the map on the screen with a pulsing blue dot. She made a finger gun with her free hand and pointed it at him.

He laughed. "You got me!" He used a Dough to Go magnet to stick the feather to the refrigerator in the kitchen. "We'll just leave that right there." He put his hat back on.

"I'm impressed. You are very sneaky, Neopolitan. It's a good thing you're on my side." He crossed his arms. "I assume that's why you're here."

She hesitated and then nodded.

"So how was school?" he asked. "Learn anything?"

He jerked backward as she swung her parasol at his face. She kept it pointed at him. Her hand was steady.

"What's that supposed to be?" he asked.

She turned and pretended to fence with an invisible opponent with the parasol.

"Is that supposed to be a weapon? Should I be scared?"

She gestured to the cane leaning against the table.

"Melodic Cudgel isn't a mere walking stick. It's a carefully crafted offensive instrument."

She shook her parasol.

"Sure, I can help you modify that," he said. "You think, what? Concealed guns are always popular."

She shook her head and jabbed with it again.

"A hidden blade. Classic." He picked up his cane. "But you'll need to know how to use it, and we may as well start with the basics."

Neopolitan showed that while she hadn't been formally trained, she had natural aptitude. She'd had some fencing lessons before, and she was light on her feet. Quick. She had excellent instincts. And she didn't hesitate to strike at vulnerable spots.

Roman went easy on her of course. She tried using her Semblance to distract him, creating a duplicate that he attacked instead of her, while she snuck up on him.

He stopped the lesson. "No tricks," he said.

She gave him a Look that suggested she thought he was crazy.

"I mean, of course tricks. But you need to learn how to fight without them first. You won't always be able to rely on your Semblance, whatever you call it, to get you out of a rough situation. Especially if you got yourself into it in the first place."

She held up her Scroll and typed. He read the word on the other side. "Overactive Imagination." He nodded. "You have a powerful skill, but it's more useful if you use it strategically. Sparingly. You want it to be a surprise—a backup plan. Not your go-to. First, you learn to fight properly. The way I did. The way I'm going to teach you."

He picked up his cane. "Again. Loser buys dinner."

This time Neopolitan avoided using her Semblance in combat, which immediately placed her higher than any of his fighting partners—none of them had ever listened to him, because they all thought they knew better than he did. Even so, she surprised him for what, the third time that night, by literally getting the drop on him with a fancy move: After he lunged his weapon at her, she hopped up onto it, and then leaped again over his head. Before he could spin and block her attack, she had whacked him in the back of the head with her parasol on her way down and followed up with a kick to his butt as she landed. He stumbled forward, but she reached out and caught the back of his jacket with the curved handle of her parasol so he didn't fall.

He straightened and smoothed out his jacket. He turned to face her. She was grinning and spinning her open parasol behind her, though it was already in tatters from their fight. She had won that round fair and square, and taught him a thing or two in the process.

"All right, then. Where do you want to eat?"

The two of them fell into a strangely comfortable rhythm over the next couple of months. Every day Neo learned new skills and fighting

techniques at school, and at night she came to Roman's to practice them on him.

Roman taught her everything he knew about picking locks, stealing cars, forgery, holdups—all the things he'd picked up on the street and from working in Lil' Miss Malachite's gang.

Finally, it was time to put everything she had learned to the test. One evening while they were training, a knock came at the door.

"Neo, if you would."

Neo looked at the door. She looked at Roman. She mimed knee-slapping, gutbusting laughter.

"Ha ha." Roman walked past her toward the door. "I simply asked you to get the door because it's for you."

She stopped laughing and pointing to herself with a skeptical expression.

Roman opened the door and picked up the long package wrapped in brown paper that was propped next to it. He closed the door and presented it to her.

"More specifically, *this* is for you," he said.

Neo took the box delicately from him. She weighed it in her hands. She shook it. She pressed her ear against it.

"Don't worry, it isn't flowers."

She stuck her tongue out at him.

"Go ahead. Open it." He sat on a stool by the counter and watched as she untied the string and peeled off the brown paper. Inside was a pink cardboard box. She shot him another glance.

He spun his seat around. "It's really not flowers."

She lifted the lid off the box and rummaged around in the pink and white tissue paper before she found what was inside. Her eyes went round like saucers and she hopped up and down. Then she pulled out a parasol.

She popped it open and admired the pink, white, and brown lacelike patterns embroidered into the light, durable fabric. She held it over one shoulder and twirled it, batting her eyelids at him.

"It's exactly as you designed it," he said. "That canopy will resist bullets, energy blasts, even small Dust explosions if you're having a really wild time."

She jumped backward and held it over her head, using the parasol to drift gracefully toward Roman.

"Yep. It can do that, too." He grinned.

She closed the parasol and swung it around experimentally. If it was anything like his own weapon, it should be weighted perfectly. Neo pressed a button and a sharp tip of a thin sword projected from the end of the parasol. Then she held the middle of the parasol and pulled out the curved black handle, drawing a rapier from the shaft. She slashed it back and forth in the air, with a rapturous expression on her face.

"I can tell that you hate it," Roman said.

Neo sheathed her weapon and leaned on it with one hand, placing the other over her heart.

"Don't get mushy on me," he said gruffly. "You needed a real weapon, now you have one. I'm really being selfish when you think about it, since I don't want you getting me killed. Do you have a name picked out?"

She closed her left eye and pressed a finger to her lips.

"Hush?"

She nodded.

"Perfect. You'll definitely shut up some people with that in your hands." He hopped off the stool. "Now for the bad news. You can't steal a bespoke like that, so I had to pay for it like some kind of rube." He'd ordered it from his favorite weaponsmith back in Mistral, Gunmetal. He didn't come cheap, especially when you were paying extra for confidentiality. "Which means . . . We're out of money."

Neo skipped toward Roman's idea board with Hush.

"That's right. Think you're ready to commit a real crime?" he asked.

She shook her head.

"No?" Roman put his hands behind his head. "You've been asking to go out and steal something every day."

She nudged Roman toward the closet and gestured for him to open it.

"Okay . . ." He opened it. It was full of clothes.

"What's all this?" he asked. "These aren't mine, officer. I've never seen them before in my life."

She pulled a hanger off the rack and held it out to him. It was a long white suit jacket with red lining and gold buttons. It was just his style and just his size. She held up another hanger with a black shirt and pants and a gray scarf.

"Where'd you get these?" he asked. "And how did you sneak them in here?"

She ignored him and pulled out another suit, white, brown, and pink. Judging by how there was significantly less fabric and it came with a corset, that one was for her.

"You made me a new outfit?" he asked.

She nodded.

Well, it would be rude not to at least try it on.

She directed him to change in his bedroom while she changed in the bathroom. They met ten minutes later in front of the mirror in his training gym.

"It looks good," Roman said.

Neo pouted.

"Great, actually. Really nice work. We look like quite a team."

She snapped her fingers, skipped away, and returned with his bowler hat. She reached into a pouch and drew out a red feather, which she stuck in the brim.

"Just a regular feather this time, yeah?" he asked.

She smiled innocently, then rose on her tiptoes and placed the hat on his head.

He sighed. "Your talents are being wasted with me. I might just regret leading you down a path of crime."

Her look said, *Don't flatter yourself.* Then she went back to his idea board, which contained sketches and scribblings of possible illegal activities, all designed to make him rich and powerful.

"So many choices," Roman said.

Neo started tearing down cards, shaking her head, crumpling them up, and throwing them away.

"Hey!" He snatched away his preliminary plans for a Doom Cannon. Not practical—yet—but he had just been doodling drawing. He just didn't know when he'd ever have a large enough supply of Dust to power a weapon of mass destruction like that. A guy needed to have dreams, though.

He picked up another crumpled plan. Then another. He started to notice a trend.

She was tossing away all the jobs that needed only one person, which didn't leave any options since he didn't exactly work well with others.

"You know, I recently had an idea for a two-person job," Roman said. "But I just don't know anyone good at both following orders *and* improvising if something goes south."

Neo waved her hand in the air.

"Are you sure you can handle it?"

She paused and put her hands on her hips, then leveled her gaze at him. She was smart enough to want to hear what he had in mind first.

"We're going to steal something that almost everyone in the city needs, artificially create a shortage. Then when people are desperate and vulnerable, we'll flood the market and charge exorbitant prices."

Neo held up her Scroll. **Dust?**

Dust. He sighed. "You aren't the first to suggest that. Maybe I should look into that, but let's stick a pin in it for now. I had something else in mind." He held his hands in the air, fingers spread. "Coffee!"

Neo made a yuck face and stuck out her tongue.

"I know, I know. But people just don't have the same attachment to tea. As soon as the people of Vale have to face a work meeting without their morning cup of coffee, we'll bring the city to its knees!" Roman clenched a fist dramatically.

Neo scratched her head.

Roman lowered his fist. "That's the beautiful part about this." He slumped down onto the couch. "I have no idea. So we get to figure it out together!"

Neo nodded and blinked her eyes. She turned the idea board to face Roman, picked up a marker, and started drawing. When she stepped away, Roman saw a cute cartoon of a Roman with an enormous head. A similarly bigheaded Neo was perched on top of him, balancing on his bowler hat with her parasol raised high.

Roman stroked his chin while he considered it. He nodded. "What could possibly go wrong?"

CHAPTER SEVENTEEN

BREWING TROUBLE

Step 1: ~~The Boring Part~~ **Reconnaissance**

Neo had no idea that planning a heist took so much time and work. *So much.* She'd always been on the impulsive side, but Roman insisted that a successful job took careful research and extensive scheming. The only way you could trust that the other members of your team were on the same page was for there to be a page in the first place. And they had to be able to read it and then follow the plan to the letter. Whenever he'd gone into a situation without knowing exactly what was going to happen, it either hadn't ended well, or it was a close call. He didn't like close calls.

Roman clearly had some trust issues to work out, but Neo was going to prove to him that he could count on her.

"First things first. We need to know where the Vale coffee warehouse is," Roman had said. "The docks probably. That's where you come in."

Where Neo came in was staking out a Magic Beans, a ubiquitous coffee franchise in Vale. She already had a brilliant disguise: a preparatory school student who had a lot of homework to catch up on. She spent three days there at a tiny table in a hard seat, drinking lukewarm, tasteless tea, before a delivery truck finally rolled up outside.

She packed up her work and hurried to the bathroom, where she used her Semblance to transform into a black-haired barista in a Magic Beans hat and apron. Then she waited near the storage area until the delivery guy appeared pushing a cart piled high with jute bags stamped with the stylized logo of the Mistral Mountains Roastery.

"Oh, hey, how's it going?" he said as he passed.

Neo shrugged.

"I know, right?" he said.

She got a good look at him and as soon as he entered the back room, she kicked the door closed and locked it. She brushed her hands together and went back to his truck. She climbed into the driver's seat and looked through all the stops on the dashboard navigation display until she found the starting point for his deliveries. She snapped photos with her Scroll and sent them to Roman.

Good work, he wrote. Head on back. And bring me a coffee—a splash of cream, no sugar.

Neo raised an eyebrow.

When she got back to Roman's apartment, he had spread out maps of the area around the coffee warehouse and blueprints of the building itself and was jotting down notes on the idea board. He reached for the paper Magic Beans cup she was carrying. She handed it over. He nearly fumbled it because it was lighter than he'd expected.

"Um." He turned the cup upside down. "Forget something?"

She pointed to the name written on the side of the cup.

"'Get your own coffee,'" he read. "Ha ha."

Step 2: Intrusion

Even after two weeks of preparation, memorizing maps of the

warehouse district, studying aerial photographs, and planning their route, Roman still wasn't 100 percent sure he was on the right building. But it matched the coordinates Neo had scored from the freight driver's truck.

"They all look the same," he muttered from the roof, looking out at dozens of identically nondescript warehouses. He didn't see how anyone could tell them apart. There was one way to find out for sure.

The good thing about all these warehouses being identical was that they were pretty much the same on the inside, too. Roman had rented one last week to assess its baseline security features and familiarize himself with its layout and weaknesses firsthand. Just like Neo couldn't get Lil' Miss Malachite's appearance right just from photo references, he didn't trust pictures and blueprints when their life or freedom was on the line.

He consulted the map on his Scroll and walked along the roof until he found the likeliest place to break in.

"X marks the spot." Roman aimed his cane down at the roof and fired a Dust flare downward. Tools might have been better suited to breaking through to the room below, with less mess and noise, but this was unquestionably the fastest way—and the ceilings weren't wired to the alarm system. Especially in the bathroom.

Roman waited for the smoke and dust to clear and then leaned down into the hole to look inside. He shone a flashlight from the back of his Scroll into the room.

Great. This was not the bathroom. It was the center of the warehouse's storage area. He couldn't make out what was inside from way up here, but the good news was he smelled coffee beans.

How had he gotten the wrong spot? He checked his Scroll and saw the map flip upside down. When he turned the Scroll over again to view it right-side up, the map flipped again.

He sighed.

May have a problem, he texted to Neo. Slight miscalculation. Blew a hole into the main area. Stick to the plan, but start the clock. Though he couldn't hear an alarm, he might have triggered a silent alert. That meant they had thirty minutes at most before the police would arrive. Less if there was any security onsite. He hadn't been able to confirm that part, but he thought it extremely unlikely. While crime organizations ran a brisk business stealing harvests from small coffee farmers in Mistral and selling them directly to distributors, here in Vale the risk was greater, with a lower chance of success.

"Why did I think this was a good idea again?" Roman asked himself. But he didn't have time to second-guess the plan now. He attached the grappling hook from Melodic Cudgel and slowly lowered himself down into the room on a wire. The doors and windows were all wired with infrared beams to detect motion, but once you were inside—like he was now—there shouldn't be any security.

As he descended, he ran through the plan again for the umpteenth time. He wasn't here for all the coffee—just the good stuff, the imports from Mistral that only came in once a month because of the distance and expense in transporting shipments, not to mention the constant danger of Grimm attacks. They could take the entire pallet in the stolen truck Neo had waiting outside the loading dock. Now that he had broken and entered, all he had to do was grab a forklift, locate the shipment, and then break and *exit*.

"Halt right there!" A voice echoed throughout the large storage space. Roman peered down and saw Roch Szalt, the Huntsman who had tried to stop him from robbing the First Bank of Vale. Former Huntsman.

"You!" they both shouted at the same time.

"You're not supposed to be here," Roman said.

"Neither are you!" Roch bellowed.

"Shouldn't you be out fighting Grimm or something?"

"They revoked my license. Because of you!" Roch grabbed his weapon and aimed it at Roman. The claw on one end of the staff hurtled toward Roman.

Roman fired a flare from the tip of the cane, which both sent Roch diving out of the way and propelled Roman on the end of his line—out of reach of the grasping claw. He used the momentum to swing himself around and around the room so Roch wouldn't be able to get a lock on him.

"Didn't take you for the kind of guy who would make a late-night coffee run," Roch said. "I was hoping it would be a quiet evening. But this is more fun."

Roman's brows knit together. It really was just one thing after another tonight, wasn't it?. He was disappointed, but not angry. Sometimes even the best laid plans needed a little bit of improvisation.

Roch spun his staff around, cocked the weapon behind him, and swung. A row of sharp spikes fanned out toward Roman. One of them smashed into his left leg. Roman grunted with pain and lost his grip on his cane, dropping ten feet to the ground. Melodic Cudgel dropped down, too, and clattered a few feet away from him.

He tried to retrieve it, but Rock's extendo-arm grabbed it first and yanked it out of reach.

"Roman Torchwick, you're under arrest," Roch said.

Step 3: Getaway

Neo drummed her fingers on the steering wheel of the cargo truck. Roman was running behind schedule. She hadn't heard from him at all since his last text message, and she was worried he was in trouble. And there was chatter on the police scanner about the warehouse—their time was almost up.

Muffled laughing came from the back of the vehicle. She had tied up and gagged the driver and stowed him back there when she took his truck. When she carjacked him, he hadn't been surprised at all. "I knew something was going down!" he'd said. "You look different, but you're that same chick from the coffee place, right? I *told* the cops to keep an eye out for a robbery."

Kidnapping a hostage hadn't been part of the plan, but he was just so annoying. She had an idea about framing him for the coffee heist but she hadn't thought that far ahead yet. She might only mess with him a little more and then cut him loose when he was good and scared.

Neo wrote another text to Roman's Scroll: It's time to go! But as soon as she hit Send, she heard a gunshot from inside the warehouse.

New plan. Neo backed the truck out of the loading dock and revved the engine. "No, no, no," the driver managed to choke out around his gag.

Yes, yes, yes. Neo floored the accelerator, and the truck lurched to life. It was slow to get moving, but once it hit a high velocity, its momentum made it unstoppable. The metal door of the loading dock crumpled like paper with a horrific shrieking and tearing sound that made her jaw ache.

She kept the truck speeding down the length of the warehouse. Up ahead, she saw Roman on the floor, bleeding. A burly man with shoulder-length white hair and silver armor loomed over him. He turned when he heard and saw the truck barreling toward him, but rather than jump out of the way, he turned to face it down. The truck hit him and his Aura flashed gray at the impact, but he was holding on to the front grille with a fierce expression on his face. He started to climb up it, his eyes locked onto Neo.

Then he and the truck smashed into a pillar in the center of the warehouse. His Aura popped and he passed out.

Good thing he cushioned the impact. The pillar began to crack and pieces of the ceiling crumbled and fell. Neo's mouth opened. *Oops.*

In the back of the truck, the trussed-up driver whimpered. He had been bouncing around the trailer as it raced around and was in even worse shape than before.

In the rearview mirror, Neo saw a forklift carrying a plastic-bound pallet of coffee headed for the truck. It pulled up alongside the driver's window and Roman leaned out.

"Need a lift?" he said.

Neo flashed him a thumbs-up and opened the cargo door. As soon as she did, the driver jumped up and ran out of the truck. Roman casually threw his cane at him, hitting him in the head and knocking him out.

"Who's your friend?" Roman asked.

She swatted a hand in the air. *Never mind.*

"Right." Roman glanced at the pillar. "When you move the truck, that thing's coming down, so I'd rather not linger. Plus, I believe I hear the distinct sound of sirens approaching. I'll load this coffee and then let's get out of here."

Step 4: Profit?

Back at Roman's they celebrated their victory with ice cream sundaes. Not only had they gotten the coffee they wanted, when the rest of the warehouse collapsed from the damage in the fight, it had ruined all the coffee they *didn't* take. It wouldn't be long before they were the only source of coffee in Vale and they could set their price.

Of all the successful heists Roman had done, this one felt the best. And maybe it was because he had come out of it richer than he'd ever expected: with a partner who could keep up with him. Better than that, Neo complemented him—and she had watched his back.

It also was nice to share this moment with someone who wasn't focused on splitting the profits. Neo was in it more for the mayhem than the money, just like him.

"Long ago I decided I never wanted a sidekick," Roman said. "But then I met you."

Neo spun and kicked him in his side. Caught by surprise, he flew across the room.

"Okay, I deserved that," he said. "What I meant was: a partner in crime."

He looked up and Neo was standing over him, offering a hand to help him up.

He took it.

CHAPTER EIGHTEEN

PANOPTI-CON

Neopolitan was having second thoughts. As much as life at the school had improved, more and more it felt like it wasn't giving her what she needed. She had already surpassed everything the teachers could give her, so she was just biding her time each day until she could start her real lessons with Roman.

Couldn't she just quit and work with him?

Unless she could come up with the information he needed to get Lil' Miss Malachite off his back, he'd never agree to that. And if she left the school, she'd lose her only insider access and her best chance at helping him. Besides, she wouldn't have anywhere else to go.

Meanwhile, it was clear that Lady Beat was becoming impatient with Neo. She wanted her to either bring Roman in herself or set him up so Melanie and Miltia could finish the job.

I need more time, Neo typed. She had used the phrase so often, her Scroll autofilled it for her.

"You have three days, or I'll expel you from this school and send you back to your parents."

Neo scowled. But she nodded and decided to step things up. And tonight was the night she was going to break into the Room. She texted Roman to cancel their usual plans.

Everything all right? he wrote back.

Just need a night in. To do the thing, she texted.

Right. The thing. Gotcha.

Then a little later, he sent: Which thing?

Neo rolled her eyes. He would either figure it out or he would understand when she gave him an update—if there was anything to update.

The Room was where Lady Beat spent all of her time when she wasn't teaching or sleeping. Neo had stumbled across it while snooping throughout the school, opening every door, every drawer, every cabinet. Some doors were locked, and Neo had managed to pick those without too much trouble. Usually they were just broom closets, storage rooms, or computer labs. But she had never been able to break into the Room.

So she had staked it out to see who was using the room, and of course it was Lady Beat. She was there almost every night, for most of the night.

But tonight, she had gone out for the evening right after class, dressed for a meeting, so this was Neo's chance to finally get inside.

Neo presented an illusion of an empty hallway while she knelt by the door and unrolled her lock-picking tools.

She laughed when she saw the lock. It was the same as the one Papa had put on her bedroom door. She hadn't been able to open it then, but she'd been practicing on locks of all types with Roman since.

Even so, it was a tricky lock, and she was nervous. It took her six tries to open it, pausing and listening constantly for footsteps.

She opened the door, slipped inside quickly, and shut it softly behind her.

The room was lit by the soft glow of a computer screen and keyboard set up on a long console with lots of blinking lights and illuminated dials.

Some kind of command station? Was this a security system for the school? But there weren't even any security cameras in the building.

Neo sat down in a comfortable swivel chair in front of the computer and tapped on the keyboard. A lock screen popped up and a light above the monitor blinked on. A camera.

"Commencing face scan . . . three . . . two . . ."

Neo quickly shifted to look like Lady Beat.

"One . . . Accepted."

The screen flashed green and a command prompt appeared. Then a holo screen appeared on the far wall opposite the door and the computer.

It was a security feed after all, broken up into squares in a 12 x 12 grid. Most of the squares were black and grainy, except for one. Which showed the computer screen she was looking at.

Neo put her hand in front of the screen and waved it. Her hand moved in the video on the holo. She brought her hand closer to her chest and moved it around until she found the camera.

The triskelion pin.

The same pin that every student at the school wore. So that was why there was no need for security cameras—they were each wearing a body cam, and sending the footage back to this viewing room.

Neo pressed the arrow key on the keyboard and the holo display shifted. More scenes, but not from inside the school. Some of these were dark as well, but several showed footage from the streets of Vale. A couple showed dinner plates, in restaurants, on a counter in a private kitchen. One showed a woman touching up her lipstick in a mirror. Neo spotted the triskelion on a brooch pinned to her black cocktail dress.

What had Roman said? His online search had shown this pin being worn by socialites all over the city, graduates of Lady Browning's Preparatory Academy for Girls. Many of them were leaders in government, executives, entrepreneurs. Partners to important people. Reporters. Bankers.

Lady Beat had an eye into some of the most sensitive secrets and private lives of people in Vale.

Neo put a hand to her mouth. This information was worth billions of Lien. It gave access to fortunes and secure servers, by showing people inputting their logins and passwords. It was a fly on the wall of important deals. And it was an endless source of blackmail material, for people who didn't want their personal business made public, or embarrassing secrets and criminal activity released to the authorities.

Neo switched back to the feed from her own camera. Now there was clear evidence that she had been to this room and knew what Lady Beat was up to . . .

Neo gasped. That's how the headmistress had known she had a connection to Roman. And because she'd been watching Neo's every move, she knew exactly what she could do, and where to find Roman.

Neo texted Roman: They know where you live. Get to safety. Don't tell me where. I'll explain later.

She had no sooner hit Send than she caught movement on the holo display. Two of the cameras were walking around the school. It was well after lights-out, and both cameras showed roughly the same view, but shifted slightly, like viewing two out-of-phase images that combined to make one 3-D image.

Two students walking side by side when they shouldn't be out of their rooms. Melanie and Miltia. And it looked like they were on their way here.

Neo dashed back to the keyboard. She had to cover her tracks.

She worked quickly, one eye on the holo display as the Malachite girls drew closer. They were climbing the stairs to this floor now.

Neo pulled up the folder directory. It looked like files were recorded in hour-long chunks organized by location, date, and another identifier. In the school folders, she found a folder marked "VAN48-1516-234-2." She tried to delete the files from the last few hours, copied in the files for the same time period from last night, and renamed them with today's date. She hoped that the system wouldn't create a new file if there was already one there, so she should be covered for the rest of the night. From there she would have to act normally until she could figure out a way to block the signal without arousing suspicion.

She was about to delete the files when she thought better of it. If she deleted the footage, even if she replaced it with footage from another night, she would tip her hand. Instead, she needed to copy this whole archive and get out. She wouldn't get another chance.

The Malachites were getting closer.

The problem was, Neo didn't have anything to copy the files with, and it would take too long to set up an online storage account—and that was traceable, too. The archive was also huge.

The Malachites' cameras showed they had reached the hallway with the door to the Room.

Neo's computer skills clearly weren't up to the challenge, but her destructive talents were. She checked under and around the console until she found an access panel at the back. She pried it open with the blade from her parasol. Inside, she found the hard drive and yanked it out, snapping ribbon cables and wires. The screen behind her glitched and went dark.

Neo shut down the display and locked the computer. She tucked away the storage drive and then stepped out of the Room. Melanie and Miltiades Malachite were right outside. They looked startled when she appeared.

"You're back already?" Melanie said.

It took Neo a moment to realize she still looked like Lady Beat.

"Is Mother here? Did you get Torchwick?" Miltia peeked around her to look inside the room. She sniffed. "Is something burning?"

Neo shook her head. She started to push past them. She had to get out of there or they'd wonder why Lady Beat wasn't talking.

"We couldn't find Vanille. She must have snuck out, too."

Neo stopped. She turned to look at Melanie.

"She's turning into quite a competent asset," Melanie said. "I'm sure Mother would like to meet her. If only to have more leverage in Vale."

Neo turned away. How did they figure that?

"Hold on. Where's your tattoo?" Melanie grabbed her by the back of her jacket and pulled down the collar. "Found you, Vanille." She yanked Neo down and backward and smashed a knee into her spine.

Neo grunted from the blow, but her Aura absorbed most of the impact. Melanie kneed her again, but this time Neo managed to twist away and shrug out of her jacket, dropping the Lady Beat illusion at the same time.

Melanie let go of the jacket as if it was burning her, and in the brief moment of distraction, Neo knocked her down with a round-house kick. She turned to run and found Miltia blocking her exit.

"Cute trick." Miltia grabbed for Neo. Neo spun so Miltia grabbed her from behind, then she slammed herself backward, knocking Miltia into the wall. Neo jabbed her elbow into Miltia's ribs and took off down the hallway. She reached the stairs, with the twins right behind her. She hopped onto the banister and waved at them as she slid down.

Melanie hurled herself over the railing and smashed into Neo, sending the both of them tumbling down the stairs in a tangle of arms, legs, and blades.

Neo's Aura burst and she lay dazed for a moment beside a similarly stunned Melanie. Miltia skated down the banister on her heels, jumped, and rolled through the air toward Neo, the knives in her heels extended.

Neo drew her parasol and opened the canopy. Miltia bounced off the reinforced fabric and landed in a crouch facing Neo.

"You should be on our side," Miltiades said. "Why stick with a loser like Torchwick?"

Neo flashed her a rude hand gesture.

"In fact, I bet he's already lost. Mother's been planning her revenge for a while. I wonder which technique she's going with."

Melanie lifted her head. She stared at Neo's bag. "She has the surveillance drive!"

Melanie lunged for it, but Neo hopped away. The girl braced on her right leg and started kicking with her left. Neo extended Hush's blade and parried her blows, edging backward toward a window.

She was still a couple stories up, but it wouldn't be the first time she'd leaped from one.

Miltiades joined the assault and Neo kept blocking and thrusting their blades. Finally, she'd had enough.

Neo held her parasol in front of her and rushed between the girls, who tried to dodge out of her way. She hooked Miltiades's wrist with her parasol and pulled her downward while the bladed tip of Hush redirected a kick from Melanie.

At the same time she launched herself so she was flipping over them and landed facing the other direction. Without the slightest hesitation she ran toward the window.

She opened Hush just as she reached the glass, which exploded outward. She jumped out and her momentum carried her away from the building in a wide, descending arc. She held her parasol aloft and it caught a breeze.

She drifted down to the ground. She saw the girls watch her for a moment before they turned and disappeared from the window. She didn't think they were going to go back to their rooms.

Together, Neo and Roman could figure out what to do with the data she had just stolen and the information about the secret spy network—but first she had to find him. And from what Melanie and Miltia had said, others were out there looking for him now.

She landed and folded up Hush. The drive was still in the bag at her side. She pulled out her Scroll to ask Roman where he wanted to meet, but he hadn't responded yet. He always answered her right away.

But according to her Scroll, the message hadn't been delivered. His own Scroll must be off, broken, or somewhere without a signal—whether it was out of range or being blocked.

If Lil' Miss Malachite and Lady Beat had found Roman, it was all her fault. She may not have known her every move was being recorded, exposing him, but she had agreed to win his trust under misleading circumstances. And she hadn't even held up her end of the bargain with him in return; if she had done more to investigate the academy, Lady Beat, and the Malachites, she might have discovered Lil' Miss's operation sooner and helped put an end to it.

Perhaps the most unsettling thing about this situation was how much she cared about what happened to Roman. Somewhere along the way, despite her duplicity, he'd become a real friend. She started running. *I'm coming, Roman!*

She wasn't going to let *this* friend disappear.

CHAPTER NINETEEN

TORCH SONG

Roman studied his crime board. The ideas were looking a little light. There weren't many opportunities left for him with Hei Xiong having so much control over the illegal activities in the city. Roman just didn't have the crew or the muscle to horn in on his territory, which just left jobs that he and Neo could handle on their own.

He rather preferred it that way. They didn't have to follow anyone else's orders. They didn't have to give any orders; in his experience, that was the real weakness in any organization. Good help was hard to find, and when you had to hire criminals to do your dirty work, they were often in it for themselves.

They made much less money that way, but it certainly seemed more fun. They were shaking things up in Vale, and it was amusing to watch the authorities and the news try to figure out why someone would steal an art print from the museum gift shop instead of the priceless original, or rob a convenience store for a six-pack of Dr. Piper.

As an added bonus, they were putting the heat on Xiong. The cops assumed he controlled all the crime in the city, so Xiong was in the strange predicament of not wanting to take credit for these bizarre crimes, nor admit that someone else was operating on his turf. That had to make him angry.

Someone pounded on the apartment door. Speaking of angry.

Roman crossed another item off his crime board and went to the door. He tried to call up the video on the intercom, but it seemed to be on the fritz. So he peeked through the peephole instead.

It was Lil' Miss Malachite.

"Ha ha," Roman said. He thought Neo had canceled their training tonight, but she probably sent that text message just to set up this prank. "That's almost perfect, but you can't fool me twice. I told you, if Lil' Miss really—"

The door bulged with bullet holes and shots filled the air. Roman dove out of the way toward the couch as the door gave way and tore apart from the gunfire. A hand reached inside and unlocked it. The door creaked open before falling off its frame.

Roman grabbed his cane from the coffee table and peered around the side of the couch as Lil' Miss Malachite stepped inside.

"Hello, Roman. Were you expecting someone else?" She fanned herself. "She won't be coming."

Roman fired his flare gun at her. She casually batted the projectile away with her fan. It hit the television and exploded, blowing a hole into his bedroom.

"Is that how we greet an old friend?" she asked mildly.

"It is after you come in shooting up my door. The condo board is going to be really upset."

She looked around. "They should be more upset with how you've decorated. That stolen painting by Madam Mauve clashes with the stolen antique vase over there. Honestly, Roman. What do they teach kids today?"

A woman stepped into the apartment. Lady Beatrix Browning from Neo's school.

"What did you do to Neo?" he shouted.

Browning tilted her head. "Young Ms. Vanille led us to you."

"And here we are." Lil' Miss smiled. "Reunited at last."

"I don't believe that." Neo wouldn't betray him like that.

"Oh?" Browning held up her Scroll and played a video. He couldn't see Neo's face because the video was from her point of view, but he saw her hands typing on her Scroll as she conversed with Browning in front of her.

"Trivia Vanille, will you help me capture Roman Torchwick?"

"You can count on me," said a mechanical voice.

"I know I can."

Neo had used him? She'd lied to him. Neopolitan wasn't even her real name. She was Trivia Vanille—which sounded strangely familiar to him for some reason.

Roman scowled. What had he expected? He'd been using her, too, or at least he'd started out that way. But he'd changed his mind, and his feelings about her. He had trusted her.

With his life, apparently.

"What do you want?" he demanded.

"I want everything," Lil' Miss said. "Starting with what you owe me."

"I spent all your money. And even if I hadn't, I wouldn't give it back."

She sat down on a high stool at the kitchen counter. She looked around disdainfully. "I'm not talking about money, dear. You know what I value most: information and loyalty."

"I'm surprised you came all this way just for me." Roman walked casually around the couch. If he knew Lil' Miss, his building was already crawling with Spiders. Even if he somehow got past her, he would have to fight his way out through the rest of them.

There was a chance he wouldn't make it, but he was a fighter, and he'd bet on himself any day. As usual, it was his supposed friends who had turned on him. He wouldn't make that mistake again.

"You have an inflated ego. I had other business here. Like you always used to say, 'If you want a job done right, you have to do it yourself.' See, I *have* learned something from you. Just as you've learned from me." She put her fan to her face thoughtfully. "We really did have some good times together."

"We sure did. Hey, since it seems my partner has betrayed me, maybe I'd be interested in putting the old team back together. What do you say?"

Lil' Miss leaned forward. "There was a time that I might have welcomed an offer like that, but I think it's clear that you aren't a good team player and you don't like sharing." She sat up. "Neither do I. However, I'm not going to kill you now."

Roman hid his relief. "You're not."

"No. I can't kill you in a tacky place like this."

"Tacky?" Roman said.

"You're coming back to Mistral with me first. I have a whole room ready for you back home."

Roman assumed his battle stance. "I'm not going anywhere with you."

"There's a time and a place for violence, but sometimes there's an easier way." Lil' Miss snapped her fan closed and a woman entered the room flanked by a couple of Spider henchman.

"Honey?" Roman said. "What are you doing here?"

"Hey, Torch," Honey Wine said. "It was nice to catch up with you a few months ago." She tipped her head to Lil' Miss. "I forgot to mention, she gave me a loan to open the Harmony Club."

"And it's coming due," Roman said.

Lil' Miss, Lady Beat, and the Spider henchman stuffed earplugs into their ears.

Honey opened her mouth and started singing.

Roman covered his ears with his hands and ran for the door, but he could still hear her and the room started to spin. He made it to the door, anyway, but one of the Spiders punched him in the chest and he doubled over. The other goon grabbed his arms and held them behind his back so he had to listen to Honey's song. The first one took his cane and the Scroll from his pocket and broke it in half.

But all things considered, he felt pretty good about what was going on. Giddy even. It felt like he was watching it happen to someone else. He forgot about why he had been trying to run, he just wanted to keep listening to the music. He followed Honey down the hall and into the elevator, swaying on his feet, almost in a stupor.

The next thing he knew, he was being tied up and tossed into the back of a van, with four Spiders guarding him. Honey raised her voice to a crescendo and when she stopped singing, he blacked out.

CHAPTER TWENTY

BOSS FOR A DAY

Neo was too late. Roman was gone.

The front door of his apartment had been blown apart. The rest of the place didn't look much better. There was a still-smoking hole in his TV and the wall it had been mounted on, and his couch was in tatters.

She found the broken halves of Roman's Scroll on the floor by the door. So that's why he hadn't responded to her messages since she escaped her school.

She sat on a kitchen stool and placed the data drive in front of her. It wasn't that big, the same shape and size of a brick. But it couldn't have been worth more if it were made of solid gold. Perhaps she could trade it for Roman; Lil' Miss Malachite would likely be upset when she found out it was gone—not just for the information it contained, but because it exposed her entire scheme in Vale.

What would Roman do if it were Neo who had been captured?

Forget about her and sell the drive to the highest bidder. And she wouldn't blame him for it. You didn't survive and get as far as he had by being sentimental.

Neo hopped off the stool. She wished she could make a backup of the drive, but she didn't have the time or the equipment. She would only get one shot at this and she had to make it count.

She hadn't meant it to happen, but Roman had been caught because of her. And she wasn't going to hide from her responsibilities any more. He was basically the only thing that mattered to her in the world right now, and she wasn't going to lose him, too.

She left the apartment building and saw the cop car she had passed on the way in was still there. Someone must have complained about the noise in the penthouse, but they didn't seem to be in any hurry to investigate. If they'd known it was Roman Torchwick's apartment and that Lil' Miss Malachite was in town, that might have lit a fire under them.

Neo was halfway down the block when she stopped and turned around. She walked over to the cop car. By the time she was next to the driver's side, both sides of her hair and both eyes were brown and she was wearing an unmodified school uniform, including the jacket she'd left behind.

The cop rolled the window down. "Good evening. Can I help you?"

Neo held up her Scroll and displayed a message: **I need to report a crime.**

The cop sat straighter. "A crime?"

His partner leaned over. "What are we supposed to do about it?"

Neo squinted her right eye. She stepped back and pointed at the Vale Police Department shield on the door. She raised her eyebrows.

The second cop laughed. "I'm just messing with you."

"Uh, what kind of crime? Are you hurt?" the driver asked.

Sort of, but that's not the point. She shook her head. She typed again. **Roman Torchwick was just kidnapped.** She pointed to the top of his building.

"What's that say?" his partner asked. "I can't read that. What's she doing with that Scroll?"

"She can't talk," the driver whispered. "She says Torchwick was kidnapped."

"Torchwick?" The partner looked at Neo. "What do you know about that crook?"

Oops. Maybe that wasn't the right approach. **Never mind. I have evidence that a crime boss has been spying on citizens in Vale. At the highest levels!!!** She hoped three exclamation points would convey the seriousness of the situation and put her hands to her head for good measure.

The partner looked around. "Is there a hidden camera? Are we being put on for a show?"

Neo rolled her eyes. *Yes, literally hundreds of hidden cameras, everywhere. That was the point.* But it was too much to type. She really missed Roman. Most of the time she didn't need to say anything and he knew exactly what she was thinking.

The exasperation must have shown on her face. The driver narrowed his eyes. "What did you say your name was?"

She started typing **Neo**, then deleted it and wrote "**Trivia Vanille.**"

"Right. One second, Ms. Vanille."

He rolled the window up and consulted with his partner while they ran her name. If not for her father, she would have had a rap sheet for all her crimes and misdemeanors before, all of which paled in comparison to the crimes she and Roman had done.

He stepped out of the car and opened the back door. "Okay. Come with us," he said.

Neo felt relieved. She doubted she could get the cops interested in saving Roman Torchwick, but they'd definitely be interested in capturing him, and bringing in Lil' Miss Malachite and Lady Beat.

But they didn't bring her to the police station like she'd expected. Instead, they rolled up to a nightclub downtown called Junior's.

Neo raised an eyebrow. Why would the police bring her here? She tightened her grip on Hush. She wasn't really worried, especially since they thought she was just Jimmy Vanille's mute and meek daughter. She would let this play out a little longer.

They marched her through the club. She hated the loud music pounding all around her. This looked like the kind of place Melanie and Miltiades would hang out, and she really didn't get the appeal.

She made note that there were a few exits, and each of them was guarded by a man in a suit with red aviators and a red tie. Similarly dressed goons, obvious members of some crime organization, were situated throughout the establishment. In fact, there were more of them than there were customers, so it didn't seem like the business was doing particularly well.

The music stopped when the cops were spotted. A tall man with a scraggly beard walked up. Neo thought he was just another bouncer until he greeted the cops by name.

"Officers Dunn and Looney. To what do I owe this pleasure?"

"We're here to see your father."

"In the back." His eyes moved down Neo's body. She gritted her teeth and concentrated on not kicking him in the face.

"She's eighteen," Officer Looney said.

"Right." The man wandered off.

They shepherded Neo through a back hallway and then through another large room—a casino. No one looked up as they passed through to another door, which led to another short corridor with a steel door at the end of it. If this were a video game, that would be the door leading to the final boss.

So Neo was a little disappointed when the door opened and she was propelled into a messy office. Behind a modest desk sat a broad-shouldered man with long, graying black hair and a bushy beard, wearing a loose pinstriped suit. He was missing most of his left ear. On his left was a willowy woman with a smart brown blazer and matching skirt. Neo noticed a familiar triskelion pin on her lapel, marking her as a Browning Academy graduate. The woman took more interest in Neo when she noticed the identical pin on Neo's lapel—both of them illusory replacements for the real thing, just for show.

"Good work, boys," the man said in a gruff voice. "See Junior for your weekly bribe."

"Do you need to call it that, boss?"

"I call it what it is. You call it whatever you want. The money will spend the same. Now leave us."

Officer Dunn patted Neo on the shoulder. "I don't know what you did, but good luck." Then he left with his partner.

Neo didn't know what she had done, either. She had done a lot of things, but she didn't know which one it was that had gotten the attention of whoever this guy was.

"Please, have a seat. Would you like something to eat or drink?"

Neo shook her head and sat down.

"You don't remember me, but I'm a friend of your father's." He pointed to a photo on his wall of him and Papa standing together outside one of Papa's warehouses on the waterfront. Judging from the amount of hair still on Papa's head, it had been taken a few years earlier.

"I'm Hei Xiong. You can call me Uncle Hei. I didn't see you around the house too often, but I used to bring you presents. Fairy tales mostly. Something told me you liked to read."

Now she remembered him. He had been at that party the last time she'd been picked up by cops in the city.

She remembered those books, too. She had wondered where they'd come from, because her parents certainly never would have thought to buy them for her. She'd particularly liked the story about the girl trapped in the tower by her evil father. She could relate, though not so much with the powerful magician coming to her rescue. If only real life were more like the stories she liked to read.

She nodded and typed on her Scroll. **Thank you. I loved those books.**

"Good. I'm glad." He smiled. "I've been looking for you for a while. That's why I had the boys keep an eye out for you, in case you turned up." He shook his head. "Your parents did a good job of hiding you."

Hiding? Neo raised an eyebrow.

"But now that I've found you, I have the leverage I need to renegotiate my deal with Jimmy. He's been cutting me out more and more, and I can't say I like it."

Neo's jaw dropped.

"I don't like to involve an innocent girl in my business dealings, but I promise you'll be treated well." He looked at the blond woman behind him. "My associate Stella will take care of you. Anything you need."

Neo stood and shook her head.

"No? What do you mean, 'No'? I wasn't asking."

That isn't why I'm here, she typed. **I have information.**

Xiong leaned back in his seat and chuckled. "She has information. Okay, whaddaya got?"

Neo looked at Stella nervously. Which was he more likely to be interested in? The data drive and the surveillance plot or Lil' Miss Malachite kidnapping Roman Torchwick?

Neo blew the bangs out of her eyes. She might as well go "all in," as Roman would say.

She held up a finger, telling him to wait a moment. This was going to take her a moment. Then she typed:

Lil' Miss Malachite has been spying on everyone in Vale using cameras hidden in alumnae pins from Lady Browning's Preparatory Academy for Girls. She used that surveillance network to locate Roman Torchwick and she kidnapped him tonight.

Xiong looked shocked. He glanced at Stella, who had taken off her pin and was staring at it.

Xiong took it from her, took out a pistol, and smashed the butt of the gun down on the pin. There was a tiny puff of smoke and

Neo smelled burnt Dust. He poked through the components with a pen and then picked up a tiny, broken lens.

"I'm so sorry, sir. I had no idea," Stella said.

Xiong clenched a fist. "What's done is done. Why should I care now, if Malachite is leaving and taking Torchwick with her?"

Neo needed him to believe her. She typed, **Torchwick has the data drive with all the business you've been conducting for the last six months on it. Malachite is going to use it to take you down and take over your operation in Vale.**

Xiong's face turned red. He was silent, and then he nodded. "Sounds like something she'd do." He pointed at Stella without looking at her. "Get the Bullhead ready. We're taking a team to go after her."

Stella hurried out of the room.

Thank you, Neo typed.

"I don't know what your whole deal with Torchwick is, but you've fallen in with the wrong crowd. Obviously. I'm going to set it right—you belong home with Jimmy and Carmel. And I'll take you back there, as soon as Jimmy agrees to my demands."

You're going to ransom me? Neo typed.

"Ransom is such an ugly word."

I call it what it is, she responded.

He laughed and wagged a finger. "You're clever all right. Jimmy always said you were a handful. I see where he's coming from. I wish I had a daughter like you instead of my idiot son."

Neo changed into his son, Junior, and winked.

"What the—?" Xiong practically fell out of his chair as he scrambled backward.

Neo stood and changed back to herself and unsheathed the

blade in her parasol. Xiong drew a gun, but she knocked it out of his hand easily and cornered him, the sharp tip pressing against the artery in his neck.

She put a finger to her lips. *Don't make a sound.*

She pulled out a pair of wrist restraints she had lifted from Officer Looney on his way out of the office and bound Hei Xiong with them.

"You aren't going to get away with this," he said.

She stuffed his tie into his mouth to keep him quiet before she changed into him, so his panicked screams were muffled. She stowed him on the couch and used her Semblance to disguise herself as him. Then she opened the door wide and found Stella waiting.

"We're ready to move out, sir," she said.

Neo nodded. She made sure Stella and the two bouncers she'd brought with her could see "Neo" sleeping on the couch. She once again gestured for them to be quiet, then pointed at the two guards and then at the door. They nodded and locked it behind her, then took up positions on either side.

Neo followed Stella through another twisty path of corridors to an elevator, which they rode to the roof. There, a small gray-and-black aircraft waited for them. Neo headed for the copilot seat.

"Sir? You usually sit in the back."

Neo fixed an intense glare on Stella and held it steady until the woman blinked. "Of course. Buckle in."

Neo carefully watched Stella's preflight sequence and everything she did to get the Bullhead up in the air. She followed along on the user manual she had pulled up on her Scroll and compared the console to the diagram.

"Where to?" Stella asked.

Neo pulled out her Scroll and opened her tracking software. It took a moment to acquire a signal from the CCTS, but soon it fixed on a pulsing blue dot, moving steadily to the east.

There you are, Neo thought. Good thing Roman never left home without his hat.

She stuck the Scroll to the dashboard. Stella gave her a skeptical look, but she adjusted course to follow the map. Thirty minutes later, she pointed down through the windshield.

"We have visual on Lil' Miss Malachite," Stella said.

Neo leaned forward and looked down. About half a kilometer below them a purple sedan was driving ahead of a convoy, which was where Roman most likely was.

"Sir? Do we engage? Once we get close enough to attack them, they'll be able to hear us. They'll know we're coming."

Neo turned and looked behind her. There were a dozen of Junior's bouncers back there, wearing helmets with red visors and combat vests, armed with machine guns. Neo waved at them and they looked at each other confused for a moment before waving back.

Then she reached for the button that would open the cargo door.

"Not that one!" Stella covered the button with her hand. "What do you think you're doing? Sir."

Neo smashed her fist against Stella's hand, pushing the button. The doors opened and the men in the back were blown out of the Bullhead.

"Oh my gods!" Stella twisted around and saw the empty cargo

hold. "Thank the Brothers they had parachutes. Why did you do that?" she shouted.

Neo dropped the Hei Xiong illusion. Stella gasped, but she was so surprised, Neo was able to reach over to unbuckle her seat belt. She pulled the woman out of her seat and tossed her into the back.

Stella managed to catch herself before she stumbled out the cargo doors. She pulled her gun and started firing at Neo. The windshield took two bullets and started to spiderweb.

Neo faced forward and pulled back on the stick, bringing the Bullhead sharply upward. She heard a shriek and when she glanced back, Stella wasn't there anymore.

Did she have a parachute? Neo wondered. She shrugged and set a course for Malachite's convoy.

CHAPTER TWENTY-ONE

FURY ROAD

Roman woke up groggy in the back of a convoy. His hands and legs were tied and he was buckled into a seat.

Slowly, through a throbbing headache, he remembered what had happened. Lil' Miss Malachite had captured him and was taking him back to Mistral.

Neopolitan had turned him over, after he had spent months teaching her everything he knew, except how to double-cross someone. She was a natural at that.

He pulled on his bonds, testing whether he could slide one of his hands free, but he'd been tied up real good. He wasn't alone back here, either. There were four Spiders guarding him, and two more in the front, one driving and another riding shotgun.

"Uh, we've got incoming," one of them said.

"Looks like one of Hei Xiong's fleet."

"Should we fire on them? They're getting kinda close."

"What's that hanging out the back?"

"It looks like . . . a girl?"

Roman's ears perked up. He craned his neck to try to look out the front window. He managed to unbuckle his seat and hop to the front.

"Get back there!" The goon in the passenger seat smacked him in the forehead with the butt of his rifle.

Roman tumbled backward. The knock on his head wasn't doing his headache any favors, and for a moment he saw stars. But he also had seen a beautiful sight: Neopolitan was holding on to a line dangling from the back of a Bullhead, paragliding with her umbrella.

I hope that thing holds out, he thought.

He heard a thud on the roof of the convoy.

"What was that?"

"The girl! She's on top of us!"

The convoy swerved back and forth on the road, bouncing Roman painfully all over the back of the convoy. One of the Spiders finally grabbed him and held him in place on the floor with a heavy boot to the groin.

"Thanks," Roman groaned.

"I'm sure we lost her," the driver said.

The footsteps on the roof proved him wrong. A clang and a sword tip appeared in the metal. It started to move in a rough circle, like a can opener.

The four Spiders in the back started firing at the roof. Roman heard an intermittent drumbeat as Neo dodged the gunfire—and then it stopped. The Spiders kept shooting for a while until it seemed like the coast was clear.

"She's hanging off the right side!" the Spider in the front called out. Then: "Hold on, she's gone. Must have fallen—"

The circular cutout in the roof fell in, and Neo landed in the center of the convoy.

"What?!" one of the Spiders shouted.

Neo quickly surveyed the situation, counting the Spiders and taking note of Roman. She moved toward him even as they tried to shoot her, swinging her parasol to deflect their guns to shoot at one another. More bullet holes appeared in the roof, sides, and floor of the convoy. The metal groaned under the stress, and the ride got bumpy again.

As Neo reached Roman, she whipped her parasol up to cut the ropes binding his feet and hands. She continued the motion to bring the parasol behind her and popped it open, just as more bullets rained down on the two of them. The reinforced canopy blocked the artillery, which bounced off and ricocheted around the cabin, causing yet more structural damage.

"Nice of you to drop in," Roman said.

Neo rolled her eyes and handed him his cane. He kissed it, then looked at Neo. "Hey, we haven't been separated for four years."

Neo tipped her head behind her.

"I know. On three."

Neo turned and put her back against Roman's, still holding her parasol up as a shield.

He counted silently, holding up his fingers so she could see them. One. Two. Three!

On three, Neo and Roman moved counterclockwise, switching places. Roman fired a flare from his cane at the Spiders and they scattered out of the way. The flare blew a hole in the side of the convoy, which shuddered and veered wide. It hit the center divider and scraped alongside it, sparks flying through the air.

The convoy jerked to the right, knocking Roman out of the

gaping hole in the side. Neo reached out for him as he fell behind the vehicle. He fired the grappling hook in his cane toward the top of the convoy and it caught on. He instantly retracted the line to pull him up onto the roof.

Neo had anchored the line from the Bullhead to the roof of the convoy. Roman grabbed on to it with one hand and then extended the handle of his cane down into the vehicle. Neo hooked the handle of her parasol around it and he lifted her up.

Neo grabbed on to the line, too, and when he nodded, she sliced through the end of it, separating it and them from the convoy. They held on tight as they lifted higher and drifted away from the road. Pieces of the vehicle were falling off and it didn't look like it would last much longer. Shots rang out at them from the passenger seat and new vantage points in the side. More shots came from Lil' Miss Malachite's ride in the front. The woman herself was watching him and Neo intently.

Roman looked up and began climbing up to the Bullhead as quickly as he could, Neo right behind him.

When they reached the aircraft's cargo area, Neo moved to the front of the ship to disengage the autolock while Roman closed up the doors.

He took a moment to catch his breath. And settle his stomach. And clutch his aching head. Then he joined Neo in the cockpit taking the copilot's seat.

"How'd you learn to fly this thing?" Roman asked.

Neo held up her Scroll.

"'How to Fly a Bullhead,'" Roman read. "You've always been a quick study."

They sat in silence for a while, which was pretty common. But this time it was awkward because there was too much that needed to be said.

But since Roman could speak, he went first. "You put another tracker in my hat."

She giggled.

"And I'm guessing you didn't actually turn me in to Lil' Miss Malachite?" Roman said.

Neo shook her head emphatically. Then she tilted her hand back and forth: *It's complicated.* She tapped at her Scroll and started sending him prewritten text messages.

Roman scrolled through the history of the text messages Neo had written that night, building a picture of what she had been through and what was at stake.

"Wow," Roman said. "So you did make a deal with Lady Browning, but you changed your mind about turning me over."

She shrugged.

"Neo, I forgive you. Trust me, I've done a lot worse. The important thing is you rescued me. Actions speak louder than words."

Neo grinned.

"Only problem is, I don't have this data drive you mentioned to Xiong."

Neo reached into her pouch and pulled out a metal brick. She tossed it to Roman and he caught it clumsily.

"Okay, then," he said. "Now what? You've pitted Xiong against Lil' Miss Malachite, and they're both going to want this data—and us. The police are working with Xiong, too. How do we turn this"—he held up the data drive—"into a winning scenario for us? Where do we even go where we'll be safe?" Even though he'd had an involuntary nap not long ago, he was exhausted. Too much adrenaline and anxiety. He needed to rest to clear his head, figure out their next move.

Neo pursed her lips. She sighed and then turned their ship south.

CHAPTER TWENTY-TWO

TWO FOR TEA

For the first time in six months, Neo saw the house she had grown up in. She'd never had a view quite like this one, of course, looking down on it from above. It had loomed larger in her imagination, but from here it was small, more like a doll's house. It was amazing what a little change in perspective could do.

"I thought we were going to your house," Roman said.

Neo looked at him. She threw her left hand out, gesturing toward the house.

"Is it behind that mansion?" he asked.

Neo put her hand to her forehead. She shook her head.

"You live there?" Roman asked.

She stretched the right side of her mouth and shrugged.

"Right. Not anymore, since you went to school."

But Neo didn't live at the school anymore, either, not after stealing the data drive and trying to expose Lady Beat and Lil' Miss's racket. If she didn't live here, either, then where did she belong?

"I'm guessing they know we're coming, since this thing makes a lot of noise. Where are you going to put us down?"

She circled the house once. They had repaired the damage to her old wing on the top floor. Like nothing had ever happened. Like she'd never even been there.

Neo brought them down on the front lawn with a jarring stop. She'd have to practice her landings. Then she just sat there.

"Let's go?" Roman asked.

The front door opened and her parents appeared. She hadn't seen them in the last six months, either. Mama stayed in the doorway while Papa stomped toward the Bullhead in his bathrobe.

"Hey! What do you think you're doing? You can't park that here!" he shouted.

Roman put a hand on Neo's arm. "You're afraid of talking to them after everything you've done in the last six months? After tonight? You jumped out of a plane tonight. You fought a group of Spiders in a moving vehicle. You faced down Vale's toughest crime boss and stole his property!"

Neo smiled and wagged her finger, then pointed at Roman.

"Right. I'm the toughest crime boss in Vale." He looked upward. "I'll remember that. What I'm getting at is you are astounding. And I'll be right there with you."

Neo blinked back tears and hugged Roman.

"Hey. Don't wrinkle the suit." But he put a hand on her head and over her shoulder, and *that* felt more like home than that house and her parents had in a long time.

Neo took a deep breath. She stood up and changed into the brown-haired, brown-eyed girl they expected.

Roman shook his head. "Show them who you really are."

Neo changed back into herself, but swapped out her school uniform for her favorite suit. Roman handed her his parasol.

They opened the cargo bays and walked down the ramp to the lawn. Papa met them there.

"I'm calling the cops! You hear me?" he shouted.

"Please don't," Roman said. "We've kind of had a rough night."

"Who—" Papa stepped closer. "Roman Torchwick! You can't be here. And you—" He turned to look at Neo. But it took him a moment to really see her. His face registered shock, sadness, and finally settled on anger. Neo folded her arms. She wasn't sure what she'd been expecting.

"Trivia! What are you doing with this criminal?" Papa said.

Neo put a hand on Roman's arm and shook her head. *He's not a criminal; he's my friend. Well, I guess he's both.*

Her father threw up his hands. "Do you know what she wants to say?" he asked Roman.

"I do, actually." Roman looked at her fondly. "I'm surprised you don't."

Defeated, Neo took out her Scroll and typed: **He's my friend. A real friend.**

Papa's eyebrows shot up. "We sent you to school to keep you from getting in trouble."

Yeah, about that . . .

Mama came running down the lawn. "Trivia! Trivia!"

She grabbed Trivia in a hug. "I've missed you! How are you? Oh, who's this?" She looked at Roman.

"That is Roman Torchwick," Papa said.

"Torchwick?" She drew away. "Here? Trivia, what is going on?"

Roman cleared his throat. "Her name is Neo."

Mama looked confused. "Neo? Neopolitan?" She looked at Trivia. "Is that what you're calling yourself now?"

Neo looked at the ground, hands folded together. She nodded.

"Well, I still need an explanation for why you're here and where you got this—" Papa gaped at the Bullhead. "This is Hei Xiong's."

"It's a long story. Mind if we, uh, crash here for the night?" Torchwick asked.

Neo jabbed him in the side with an elbow.

"Okay, okay, the landing wasn't *that* bad."

"This is Trivia's home," Mama said. "She's always welcome here. And her friends. We'll have plenty of time to sort all this out once you've had a chance to rest."

Neo felt a tiny surge of warmth and affection at her mother's words. She hadn't heard from her parents since she'd been enrolled at the academy, so she had assumed they had all but forgotten her.

Papa nodded distractedly. "Yes . . . Of course. It's good to have you home, Trivia."

She forced a smile. Neo had become better at reading people in her time at the academy. She knew Papa was hiding something. But it wasn't like she and Roman had any better option at the moment. They just needed to recover a little, and then they could move on.

"Probably won't be long before someone finds this." Roman kicked the side of the aircraft. "And us."

"Who's looking for you?" Papa asked. "I have a right to know if you're under our roof."

Roman walked toward the house. As he passed her father, he tipped his hat. "Oh, everyone really. Take your pick."

Neo shrugged and ran after him.

"Sooo . . . You're rich," Roman said, lounging on the sofa beside her with his feet up on the antique coffee table. Even now, the gesture made her wince; she sat on the edge of the cushion, back straight, trying not to touch anything. She had been punished just for playing in this room as a kid; it was used only for her father's business meetings, guests like Hei Xiong apparently.

"You could have mentioned that at least once, maybe before we went out to steal something you probably could have put on Daddy's credit card." He nodded at her parasol. "You could have paid for that by yourself."

Neo shot him an annoyed look.

Roman put his hands up in surrender. "Sorry! I know it isn't your money. Yet." He winked. "But it's still a lot to take in. There is a giant portrait of you on that wall right behind you and it is kind of freaking me out."

Neo hated that painting. It showed her and her parents posing together as if they were a happy family. But it was all a lie. Right down to the two brown eyes on twelve-year-old Trivia. For all her parents' criticism of her imagination, it was them who had been living in a fantasy.

"You were a cute kid. What happened to you?"

Neo sighed.

"I'm kidding. Come on, you're usually the fun one. Being back here really bothers you, huh?"

She glanced up to the ceiling. That was an understatement.

Roman kept staring at the family portrait. "There's something off about this picture."

Neo waved her hand and fixed the color of her right eye in the portrait.

Roman snapped his fingers. "Much better."

Neo's mother and father came in. Mama carried a tray with a teapot, teacups, and Neo's favorite little cakes. Neo was surprised they still had those around when she wasn't even home.

"Tea?" Mama asked. The glasses rattled on the tray. Her hands shook and she was squeezing the handles of the tray so hard her knuckles were white. Neo didn't know why she was so nervous; Roman wasn't the first criminal she had entertained in her home.

"Absolutely. Thanks, Mrs. Vanille. I'm starving," Roman said.

"Please, call me Carmel." Mama poured tea, sloshing a fair bit of it out of the cup. He picked up the cup and showed it around so everyone knew he was holding it properly with his pinkie sticking out.

Neo sipped her tea sullenly. She made a face. Tea usually made everything better, but even this tasted wrong somehow. Too bitter.

It was very strange to have Roman here with her parents. Like her two worlds were pulling at her. She was starting to feel more like Trivia than Neo again, and it was unsettling.

She didn't want to stay here.

Mama and Papa exchanged uncertain glances.

"You can stay the night, Torchwick," Papa said. "Tomorrow morning you will leave, without our daughter."

Neo looked at Roman in alarm. He glanced at her, and then he downed the rest of his cup and threw it against the wall.

Neo flinched at the sound of breaking glass. She looked at her parents worriedly. What were they going to do?

"That was unnecessary." Mama wrung her fingers together.

"We can't harbor criminals here," Papa said.

Neo laughed, but it came out sounding like a hiccup. Everyone looked at her.

She pointed a finger at her dad.

"What are you implying?" Papa asked angrily.

She transformed into Hei Xiong for the second time that night. Her father visibly recoiled.

Roman watched all this with interest. "You're in with the Xiong family, eh?"

"I manage business contracts for the city," Papa said. "That requires me to deal with a lot of people."

"Then you're definitely in with them. Every businessman works with him or for him—or he has something on them. What does Xiong have on you? Kickbacks, I bet. Giving him insider knowledge? Plum deals? You made him the biggest Dust distributor—"

"That's enough!" Jimmy said.

Roman looked around. "City employees typically don't live this good. Which is why they all work with the crime syndicates." Roman put his fingers and thumbs together to make a circle. "The circle of life."

"How dare you." Papa advanced toward Roman, but Mama held him back.

"I will not be lectured in my own home by a low-rent crook!"

"Low rent? My rent is at the top of the scale for Vale, and it's probably going to get higher because of the damages."

Neo narrowed her eyes. Papa was right: He didn't have to put up with this kind of treatment. Which begged the question, why *wasn't* he doing something about it? She cocked an ear, listening for sirens or the roar of a Bullhead's engine. Maybe he wanted to keep them talking for some reason . . .

She slammed her cup down on the table and it split in two. The remainder of her tea pooled around the broken halves. She stood and gestured to Roman. *Let's go.*

"You sure?"

Neo nodded. Or tried to, but she couldn't get her head to move. Her eyes flew open in panic. Her face abruptly felt numb and she couldn't feel her hands and feet.

"Neo?" Roman asked. "Neo!"

She tried to take a step, but it felt like weights were tied to her leg. She barely moved her foot an inch before she was falling over. Papa caught her and held on tight.

From this angle, she saw that Roman was similarly paralyzed on the couch, a look of concern frozen on his face. Concern for her.

And then Papa started dragging her away.

CHAPTER TWENTY-THREE

MEETING THE PARENTS

Roman watched Jimmy Vanille haul his own daughter out of the room, furious. He wanted to stop him, but he couldn't. Not yet.

He followed Carmel Vanille with his eyes around the room as she tidied up. She went to pick up the shards of the broken cup Roman had thrown across the room and tsk tsked over the spilled tea on the carpet and the walls.

"You've clearly been a bad influence on Trivia," she said. "She was always a sweet girl."

Roman made a sound like a choked laugh.

"She had her problems, but what girl doesn't?" She looked at the painting on the wall with a wistful expression. With Neo out of commission, it had reverted back to its original state—an idealized portrait of a family for a woman who had lost touch with reality.

Naturally that meant Hei Xiong's Bullhead was visible for anyone looking for it. Their time here was short.

Carmel whirled around. "You think we don't know who you are, Torchwick? You think we don't know what's going on in our daughter's life, even when she isn't here?"

She lifted the chain around her neck and showed him the pendant dangling from it. A triskelion.

Roman groaned inwardly. Neo's mother had graduated from Lady Browning's Preparatory Academy for Girls, too. No wonder she had shipped her daughter off there.

And it seemed that she was a bit more involved in Lady Beat's plans than most of her former students. In fact, he wondered if Jimmy knew his wife had been using him to spy on Hei Xiong's operations.

But Roman couldn't ask any of the questions spinning around in his head. Fortunately it seemed Neo's mother didn't have any trouble talking.

"We were in deep," she said. "Deeper than we should be. Jimmy didn't want to be under Hei's thumb forever. He wanted to start a little side business, and, well, you know how that goes." She looked at Roman. "Here you are."

She straightened a chair that had been nudged maybe half an inch when Neo had stumbled and been pulled away.

"I tried to change his mind, but Jimmy never listens to me." She rolled her eyes, in a very Neo way. "I'm just supposed to look pretty and smile a lot. Which is harder work than you think. But I was trained for that. 'Be seen but not heard, that's living the dream,' as Lady Beat drilled into us. 'The better to watch and learn, and plot and scheme.'" She laughed. "Jimmy has no idea what's really going on. He never did. I knew what Trivia needed, but he wouldn't let me give it to her. He didn't want her to grow up like him." She chuckled. "But that was going against her nature."

Carmel approached the couch. Roman felt his already sore

muscles tighten. She slid his legs off the coffee table and frowned at the marred surface.

"Lady Beat will be pleased when I return the data drive you stole. And when I hand you over to Lil' Miss Malachite, I'll make sure she gets Hei off our backs once and for all. With him out of the picture, the Dust trade will be up for grabs, and Jimmy will rally the council to give him emergency power over the Dust imports, distribution, and sales." She winked. "But we know who'll really be in charge, don't we?"

In one fluid motion, Roman grabbed her, taking her by surprise, holding her arms at her side with one arm and covering her nose and mouth with the other.

"You talk too much," Roman said.

She struggled, her screams muffled, but she couldn't break his grip. Gradually she stopped fighting him as she ran out of oxygen and passed out.

He dropped her on the couch. "Thanks for the tea, but one of the first things I learned on the street is to be careful about what you eat. I didn't have to go to a fancy school for that one."

He grabbed curtain pulls from around the room and tied her up with them. Then he waited by the door for Jimmy to come back.

He walked into the room completely oblivious to his unconscious wife, texting on his Scroll.

"Darling, Hei is on his way over here. Once I give him this data drive and Torchwick, he says all my debts are forgiven. I can't believe this opportunity dropped right into our laps. Isn't that splendid news?" Jimmy looked up. He saw his wife.

"I've heard better news," Roman said.

Jimmy spun around, reaching into his pocket, but Roman whacked him on the head with his cane. Jimmy went down.

Roman checked the man's pockets and relieved him of a pistol and the data drive. Roman weighed the thing in his hand.

This information was hot, but it wasn't the kind of thing that increased in value the longer you held on to it. Some of it would still be damning evidence, but the real usefulness of it was in the current deals going on, which must be why Xiong and Lil' Miss wanted it so badly. Maybe even more than they wanted Roman.

He might be able to make a deal and get out of this one . . . But then what? They'd come after him eventually, and what he really wanted was to eliminate both of them as a threat so that he could take over. And there was probably only one way to do that. And if he was going to do it, he needed to do it quick before they had company.

But first, he needed to find Neo.

CHAPTER TWENTY-FOUR

FALLING IN

A *Few Minutes Earlier . . .*

Neopolitan had never seen her house from this perspective before, either, being dragged backward through the halls by her father. Her heels left scores in the varnished wood floors.

Sorry, she thought immediately, and then wondered why she was apologizing. It wasn't her fault, and she had no control over this situation.

An uncomfortably familiar feeling for her.

"I know what you're thinking," Papa said, huffing as he pulled her up the main stairs.

That would be a first. He hadn't even heard of some of the curses she was yelling at him internally.

Neo's mind flailed around in her paralyzed body. Her tongue had never done what it was supposed to, but now the rest of her was traitorous. Useless.

She was a prisoner in her own body.

"What is my father doing?" he went on. "What I've always done, kid. Doing what's best for my family. For you. Trust me, you don't want to get mixed up with Roman Torchwick and the dangerous world he lives in. It changes you."

Is that what happened to you?

He paused halfway up the stairs to catch his breath. "It started out small enough. Hei Xiong offered me an incentive to make sure the contract for Dust transportation in the city went to his family's business. I didn't see any harm in it, making a little extra money. They were a good business. And Xiong's a good person to have on your side." He scowled. "Which isn't to say he's a *good* person. Far from it."

He lifted Neo up again and groaned. "I guess you've been eating well at that school of yours." He chuckled.

Excuse me?

"That first job turned into other offers, some of which I was less comfortable with. Higher profile projects, more vendors competing for the same contracts, more interests to factor in. But you don't say no to Hei Xiong. Meanwhile, the price for yes kept getting higher."

He stopped, staring into space. His nostrils flared. "And when things got rough, Xiong was always there to 'help.' Pretty soon I owed *him* money. I had to put myself more and more on the line to pay him back, stay in his good graces." He lowered his voice to a harsh whisper. "Embezzling. Taking bribes. Stealing from—" He caught himself and his eyes went back and forth wildly. "Shhhh. Shhhh . . . They have ears everywhere."

Eyes too, Neo thought.

They continued up and when he reached the landing, Papa looked around. "Xiong owns all this, did you know that? He owns me. He owns your mother. He owns you. But now, thanks to you I have something he wants. I can wipe my debts clean. And this time, I'm coming out on top."

He dropped Neo to the floor with a thud.

Ow.

They were outside her bedroom—what had been her bedroom. But the wooden door had been replaced with a steel one, and there was a hand scanner now connected to a complicated lock that would take her weeks to crack. She wondered what was so important enough to need all that security.

The door opened with a *whoosh*, and he picked her up again. He backed through the doorway, sliding her over the threshold and along the floor. It looked like her old carpet.

He pulled her alongside a canopy bed and hauled her up into it. He rolled her onto her back and arranged her hands across her stomach in a funereal pose.

Then he reached into her pouch and pulled out the data drive.

"I'll be back after Xiong takes this and that crook away. We can have a family dinner again, just like old times."

Yeah, right.

"Don't go anywhere." He chuckled. He kept laughing, growing louder and louder as he switched off the lights and closed the door with a hiss and definitive *kerthunk*. The soundproofed door finally cut off his manic laughter, and Neo was left alone with her thoughts.

She didn't know how long she lay there, staring up at the canopy of her bed in the dark and silence.

Is this what it's like to be dead?

She waited.

After some time had passed, a patch of light crept along the ceiling and she heard the crunch of a car in the gravel driveway.

She waited.

Another set of lights, coming in faster. Tires squealing. Gunfire. There was a war going on outside her window.

She thought about all the things she was going to do to her parents when she escaped from here.

She thought about what life might be like after this, if she and Roman somehow survived this. If their friendship survived this.

She wondered if she would ever be free again.

Eventually she felt a painful tingling in her extremities. She wiggled her fingers and toes experimentally. She was getting her mobility back.

She still couldn't feel much, but that hadn't stopped her before. She forced herself to sit up, nearly tipping over in the bed, and swung her legs down to the floor. She pushed herself off the bed to see if they would hold her weight.

Not yet. But she could crawl. It felt like swimming in sand and it hurt, but she made it to the window and looked out.

Lil' Miss Malachite's forces and Hei Xiong's were trading gunfire from behind their vehicles. They were also shouting at each other, likely trading insults, but she couldn't hear them through the glass. She pounded on the window, but it had been reinforced with an Atlesian hard light force field. There'd be no jumping out of it this time.

She pulled herself up and stumbled over to the door, more falling than walking. She couldn't even pierce the steel door to get to the locking mechanism if she wanted to. She tried banging on the door, but her fists didn't even make a sound on the metal.

She sat down and looked around her room. It was a mostly

faithful recreation of her bedroom, with the same furniture: the bed, the dresser, the bookcase. But it was empty of her belongings. There was no personality. No one lived here.

Which was strange, because if she didn't live here, why go to the trouble of restoring her room? Why put a heavy-duty lock on the door and an expensive force field on the window?

You didn't do that to keep someone in. Those were security measures to keep someone out. And only one person had access to the room that she knew of.

The door mechanism whirred. Neo moved fast, as fast as she could manage with her laggy body. She grabbed her parasol from where it had fallen under the bed and extended the blade, pointing it at the door, prepared to rush Papa as soon as it opened.

Whoosh. The door opened and Neo launched herself.

"Whoa!" Roman dropped something and dove out of the way as Neo embedded her sword in the opposite wall. Mama wasn't going to like that, either, but Neo had never liked the wallpaper.

She turned toward Roman and put her hands over her heart.

"Ah, don't get mushy. You would have done the same for me."

She looked off into the distance, her mouth pushed up thoughtfully.

"Yeah. You did do the same for me. But who's counting? We're a team, right?"

Neo grinned. She had really thought she would be trapped in there and would never see Roman again. But how had he gotten inside the room without—

She looked down and saw Papa's limp body on the floor. She put a hand on her hip and gestured at him.

Really?

"He's not dead," Roman said.

Neo studied her father. Just a little while ago he had drugged her and then locked her in a room, claiming it was because he wanted to protect her. But from here, it looked like he had been trying to protect himself. She hadn't felt any emotions when she thought about him being dead. Not sadness, or joy, or disappointment. No fear, no love. Perhaps he had been distant with her for so long, she now felt the same about him.

"I looked all over the house for you. There must be forty rooms in here," Roman went on.

She flashed five fingers at him, and then one hand and one finger.

"Fifty-six, then. For three people! That's a lot. And every one of them is filled with expensive junk. No wonder your dad is broke. Anyway, I finally found this door, and it was clear there was something important behind it." He gestured to Neo. "A father's greatest treasure, that kind of thing. But seriously, I've seen weaker security in a crime boss's personal vault. I had to go all the way back upstairs and grab the guy so I could use his handprint to open the door."

Neo unsheathed her sword blade and pointed to Papa's hand. She made a hacking motion and then lifted a brow.

Roman stared at her. "See, this is why I need you around."

Neo crouched down and went through her father's pockets. She came up with her Scroll but there was no sign of the data drive. Roman saw her frustration.

"Don't worry, I've got the drive. And I've been trying to figure out what to do with it. Look, there's a lot you need to know, but we don't have time right now. It won't be long before Lil' Miss and Xiong decide they should work together to break in and capture us." He paused. "You hear that?"

Neo listened but she didn't hear anything. She pretended to clean an ear with one finger.

"Exactly. They've stopped fighting. Which is bad news for us, because—"

Several floors down they heard banging at the front door. Broken glass.

"I think the only way to get them off our backs is to turn the heat up on them," Roman said.

Neo nodded. She typed on her Scroll. **What do you need?**

"A computer," he said. "And a distraction."

She propelled Roman down the hall to her father's office. This door was locked, too, but it was just a normal door, a normal lock. Which she kicked in with her normal boot.

She and Roman piled into the office. He fired up the computer and groaned when he saw the password screen. The camera above the screen lit up.

"Be a dear and go fetch your father's head, will you?" he asked.

Neo shuddered with a grimace. She transformed into her father and let the computer scan his face. The screen lit up.

Roman sat at the desk and started plugging cables into the data drive. "I think I can get this to work, but it's going to take a while, and even longer to upload it all."

Neo caught her reflection in the mirror over the credenza. Her father's face looked back at her. She wondered how he became the type of person to risk losing everything to get what he wanted. She wondered if she would make the same choice.

She thought about how angry he'd been when she set that fire. "You could have blown us all up," he'd said. It had seemed like an exaggeration.

But what if it wasn't?

Neo bolted out of the room.

"Don't worry, I'll be fine!" Roman called. "Just keep them off my back!"

She ran down the hall toward her room. Her dad wasn't lying there anymore. She slowed down and crept more slowly and quietly. She shifted her form until she looked like she had at age six, playing sneak tag with her invisible friend.

She peeked around the edge of the door into the room. Her bed was shoved to one side, and Papa was pulling long boxes out of a crawl space under her floor.

What?

He was muttering to himself. "I'll give it all to them; it's the only way. The only way."

His head jerked up and he saw her by the door.

"Trivia?" he asked. "Sweetheart, you didn't leave! Come here, help me with this."

Neo approached warily, so she could get a look at what he had stashed under her bed: crate after crate of Dust crystals.

Neo's mouth fell open. She pointed at it all and then spread her hands in a question.

"I've been setting this Dust aside for some time. It's our nest egg." He squinted. "Did you change your hair?"

She didn't bother with the Scroll this time. She made her question appear in the air in front of her, floating between her and her father.

In my bedroom?

He stuck his hand into a box and pulled out a handful of small red gems. Burn Dust.

"If Xiong ever found out I'd been stealing from him, he wouldn't be able to prove it if he couldn't find it. No one would ever think to look in your room." He tapped his forehead. "I'm smarter than your mother thinks! She underestimates me. Xiong underestimates me! But I had everyone fooled for all these years."

He frowned at her. "Until you messed it all up. First you started that fire, right on top of all this valuable Dust!"

Neo swallowed, the hairs crawling on the back of her neck. The Dust wasn't just valuable, it was incredibly volatile. She'd been sitting on top of a massive bomb that would have leveled the whole neighborhood. If the fire had sparked it, she never would have known what hit her.

She was still standing on a bomb, but in this case it was Papa who was unstable.

He jumped up. "Then you and Torchwick arrived. Were you looking for this? How did you know about it?"

Neo held out her hands, more in warning to him than out of fear. She changed back into herself and backed away slowly.

"You're a witch, just like the ones in those silly stories you read." He stalked toward her.

Neo held up a match and ignited it with her thumbnail. He froze.

She smiled and tossed it toward the box of Dust. As he dove to catch it, she whirled around and fled the room for the last time in her life. She slammed the door on him and leaned against it, breathing heavily. The machinery whirred and rumbled against her back as the locks engaged. She relaxed her Semblance, making the illusory match fade.

She heard muffled thumping on the door. But Papa was the only one who could let himself out.

CHAPTER TWENTY-FIVE

SMOKE AND MIRRORS

Roman was no computer genius, but because he didn't trust others to do his dirty work for him, he knew just enough to be dangerous. And when it came down to it, he was fine with poking and trying things until something worked. Fortunately, the data drive seemed fairly plug and play, and soon he was clicking through folder after folder of incriminating and private videos.

He wished he had some popcorn and a big-screen TV to scroll through the good stuff, but what he really needed was time and a good way to get this stuff out to the public.

So he called the Vale News Network.

"I have a hot scoop for Lisa Lavender," he said when some intern answered.

"It's the middle of the night," the woman said.

"Something new is always happening. That's why it's news."

"I'll take a message."

"You will connect me to her right now, or I'll take my news elsewhere. But she's going to be extremely upset to miss out on the story of the century."

"That's quite the hyperbole," she said.

"Well, it's certainly the biggest thing to happen in Vale all week."

"Who is this, anyway?"

"Roman Torchwick."

She paused. "*The* Roman Torchwick?"

"The very same."

"I've never heard of you."

Roman sighed. "Well, Lisa has. So get her on the phone right now."

A text message came in from Neo: They're in the house. I'm leading them to the Dust cache in my bedroom. That should distract them while we get away.

The WHAT cache? Roman texted back.

Papa's been stealing Dust from Xiong's shipments for years and hiding it in my room. Try to keep up.

Hei Xiong would definitely want that back. Lil' Miss Malachite wouldn't turn up her nose to a small fortune in Dust, either.

Roman wanted it, too. But if it was a matter of life or Dust, well . . . He'd have to think about that more.

"This is Lisa Lavender." A voice broke in on the line.

"I recognize your voice from TV."

"Is this really Roman Torchwick?"

"It is."

"What have you got? I'm a big fan . . ."

Roman smiled.

"Of ratings. And it's not every day that a criminal mastermind calls me."

Roman nodded.

"So I'll take what I can get," she continued.

Roman scowled. "Do you usually roast your informants like this?"

"Oh no," she said. "I'm just trying to keep you busy on the line while the police trace your call."

Roman slapped his forehead. "I do actually have information for you that I think the police will be interested in, too."

"Let's hear it."

"Lil' Miss Malachite has been spying on people in Vale using cameras hidden in triskelion pins worn by women in very high security positions."

Lisa Lavender was quiet for a long moment.

"Well?" Roman said.

"Sorry. I, um, just had to throw something out. You were saying. Do you have proof?"

"A whole data drive worth of it, ready to beam to your server."

"Okay, I'll have someone text you an address and password." She cleared her throat. "And Roman?"

"What?"

"I loved the flowers."

Neo figured Roman would be a bigger target for Lil' Miss and Hei Xiong, so she took on his form and worked her way downstairs. They weren't as quiet as she was, and she knew every nook and cranny—except the secret one in her own bedroom, apparently. It was a simple matter to sneak around and subdue the Spiders and Xiong's men, who of course had split up to search the house.

She encountered Lady Beat and Hei Xiong in the parlor, standing over Mama's body. Lil' Miss wasn't with them. Mama was tied up, but Neo couldn't tell if she was still alive or not.

Neo stopped to think about how she felt about that. Should she try to save her mother or leave her to face whatever fate awaited her with her fellow criminals?

Her Scroll buzzed. You good? I'm all set here. The files are transferring. We should go.

Wait for my signal, Neo sent back.

Roman was counting on her. She darted out from the doorway and dashed across the room.

"It's Torchwick!" Xiong shouted.

Neo heard his footsteps behind her. She doubted Lady Beat would be able to keep up.

Xiong followed her all the way up the stairs, firing shots after her. She got to the top floor first.

Roman heard gunshots in the house and Xiong bellowing his name.

"That would be Neo," he said. The files were done transferring, so the data drive itself now was almost worthless. It was almost time to go.

He sat down again and pulled up Jimmy Vanille's files. He was responsible for pulling a lot of strings in the city, so he had to have something interesting on there.

Something like spreadsheets, contacts, manifests, and information on deals above and below board. Roman grinned. This could be worth almost as much as what he'd just given up. He copied the contents over to the data drive and slid it back into his pocket.

He snuck into the hallway and saw Hei Xiong standing there, pointing his gun at—Roman Torchwick.

Neo appeared next to Roman and made him jump. She gave him a Look.

"What took *me* so long? I'll show you later," he said.

Neo grabbed his arm and pulled him toward the stairs.

"Got nothing to say now, huh, Torchwick?" Xiong said.

Roman opened his mouth. Neo shook her head. At the moment that Xiong fired his machine gun at the duplicate Roman, they bolted down the stairs. Xiong's cursing followed them down.

"He'll be happier once he finds that Dust," Roman said.

They reached the first floor and headed for the front door. Roman opened it.

"Coast looks clear," he said.

A moment later, a spotlight shone on them. He shielded his eyes and peered out as Neo grabbed his other hand.

A Bullhead was hovering over the lawn, its spotlight and guns trained on them. In the illuminated cockpit, he saw his old friend Brick at the controls, with Lil' Miss Malachite herself sitting beside him.

"I guess this is it," Roman said. It was the end of the line.

Neo squeezed his hand. He glanced at her and was surprised to see Carmel Vanille in her place.

"Neo?" Roman asked.

He glanced down at himself and saw he was wearing Jimmy Vanille's tacky suit and shoes—and presumably his face.

Neo tugged him forward and they walked down the stairs and along the path slowly toward a car parked in the driveway. The spotlight followed them. He looked nervously up at the Bullhead. Lil' Miss was watching them closely.

"I'd be surprised if she let us go," Roman said. "Unless you can hold these disguises indefinitely, once they capture us they'll figure out who we are."

Neo's brows knit together, either from concern or concentration.

"We need to give her a bigger target, something she wants enough to draw her attention while we get away." He stopped walking. "While *you* get away. She's mainly interested in me. Drop this disguise and I'll distract her. You get out of here. And never look back."

She shook her head defiantly. He tried to pull his hand free, but she only held on more tightly.

The Bullhead moved toward them slowly. He could be wrong. Lil' Miss might just decide to cut her losses and write this whole thing off as a botched job—wipe out all of them from spite and just to be sure everyone who knew about her operations in Vale was no longer a threat.

"Please. You have to let go."

Neo's chin trembled. She glanced back at the house and then up at Roman's face.

Then she started waving frantically at the Bullhead.

"Neo?" What was she doing?

For a moment he wondered if she was going to turn him in and try to strike a deal for herself. Which he couldn't really blame her for trying. He even kind of expected it, given his track record with partners. Another day, another Roman might have done the same. Anything to survive.

Neo stared down the Bullhead—stared down Lil' Miss Malachite—and pointed up at the house. Lil' Miss turned to look.

Roman couldn't believe it when the ship slowly turned away from them to face the house. She had taken the bait. But what was the bait?

The spotlight illuminated the upper corner of the house. Two figures were visible in a third-floor window. Their backs were turned, but they were clearly him and Neo. The figures turned to look out at the Bullhead. The fake Roman flashed a rude gesture and fake Neo stuck her tongue out.

Neo dropped Roman's hand and started running toward her father's car in the driveway. Roman followed her lead. She looked like herself again, unable to maintain multiple illusions, and not really needing to now that the attention was off them, for the moment.

When Neo reached the car, she opened the driver's side door and climbed inside. Roman hopped into the passenger side. She was too short to see over the steering wheel.

"Do you need a booster seat?" Roman asked.

She glared at him. He raised his hands innocently. Then he heard gunfire from the Bullhead as Lil' Miss began attacking the window, trying to kill him. The window was holding up shockingly well, thanks to a hard light force field blocking the bullets.

"It's shielded?" Roman said.

But the walls around the window weren't, and they were crumbling under the gunfire. The guns stopped.

Neo buckled her seat belt. She tapped his leg. Roman ignored her and kept watching as the Bullhead fired a missile, which finally broke through the hard light force field.

Then he got it. That room was protected because it was where Jimmy Vanille had been stockpiling Dust.

Roman grabbed for his seat belt and fumbled blindly with the clasp—

Too late. There was a brilliant flash of white light followed a moment later by a tremendous boom and crack of thunder. Then the shock wave came, tearing through the mansion. The Bullhead lost control and came down beyond the driveway, just past the tree line.

When the force hit the car Roman and Neo were in, it pushed the vehicle into the air. It turned over and over until it finally came to a rest on the other end of the driveway.

CHAPTER TWENTY-SIX

FRIENDS TO THE END

Neopolitan staggered out of the crumpled car. Her Aura was almost depleted, but she was all right.

She checked on Roman. He had been thrown clear of the vehicle as it tumbled through the air and was lying on his back on the lawn. He was unconscious but breathing. Unfortunately his hat wasn't going to make it. He had landed on it and crushed it.

Neo looked over at her house, or what was left of it. The explosion of all the Dust packed in her room had leveled the top two floors of the house, and the first floor had collapsed in on itself.

She sat beside Roman and watched the sun rise behind the rubble. She heard sirens in the distance.

Roman gasped and sat up. His eyes squinted in pain. "Wow," he said when he saw the remains of the house. "Did anyone make it out of that? Xiong?" He hesitated. "Your parents," he said softly.

Neo shook her head. Papa had been locked in that room, at the epicenter of the detonated Dust. He'd been killed by the only thing he'd truly cared about: his ambitions.

And killed by his daughter.

Lil' Miss might have been the one to pull the trigger, but Neo had pointed her guns at her father. And Mama . . .

Roman paused. "You all right, Neo?"

She shrugged. She really didn't know. But she wasn't not all right.

As far as she was concerned, Trivia Vanille was buried under that mess, too. Neopolitan was the sole survivor. With her parents gone, she didn't have anything or anyone to run from anymore.

She was finally free.

"You know, I lost my parents when I was younger than you, and I turned out okay," Roman said in a lighter voice.

Neo looked at him and cracked a smile. He caught a lock of her hair and showed it to her. It was white. "This is new. It suits you," he said.

Why would she have done that with her Semblance?

The sirens grew louder. "Soon this place is gonna be lousy with cops, reporters, fire brigades." He glanced at the destroyed car behind them, then at the Bullhead they had flown in on. "Think we can get that junk heap back in the sky?"

Neo and Roman trudged toward it side by side.

The Bullhead, already riddled with bullets, its windshield shattered and gone, had sustained additional damage from the explosion, but most of the preflight checks turned up green, and whatever that red light was, she would deal with it later.

"You . . . can just drop me wherever," Roman said.

She shot him an anxious look.

"Unless you want to stick together?"

She gave him a look that she hoped expressed how incredibly clueless she thought he was. *Dum-dum.*

"Can't imagine why you want to hang out with someone like me. With your abilities, you could be anything you want—even a Huntress."

Neo burst out laughing. She turned to him and briefly transformed into Vale's most famous Huntress, Glynda Goodwitch. She saluted him.

Can you imagine that?

"Maybe not," Roman said. "But the criminal world isn't ready to deal with you yet. I mean, I'm still not interested in having a sidekick—" She glowered.

"But I couldn't ask for a better partner."

Neo leaned over and kissed Roman on the cheek. His face went red. It was fun to mess with him sometimes. She tousled his hair for good measure. He needed a new hat.

"Stop," he said, pulling away.

Neo quickly returned to the controls and started to raise the Bullhead.

"It's a shame we literally blew a fortune in Dust," he said. "But there's more where that came from." He patted his pocket. "For all his many faults, your father had a decent plan. Control all the Dust in the city, and you control everything else. It's just too bad he didn't have you helping him make it work. But with Hei Xiong out of the picture, and Lil' Miss retreating to Mistral, we're the only game in town."

Neo frowned. She didn't really care about running things, or cornering the market on Dust. She just wanted to do whatever she wanted. And for the moment, what she wanted was to help Roman set the world on fire.

Once they were at cruising altitude, Neo looked at Roman. *Where to?*

He grinned. "Your choice."

On the horizon she spotted other ships on their way from the city center. That decided that—she steered them in the opposite direction, at full throttle. She leaned back in her seat and closed her eyes, feeling the warm sun on her face and the wind blowing through her hair. For once, she wasn't worried about anything.

No one was ever going to catch Roman and Neo.